Charles G. Leland

**English-Gipsy Songs**

In Rommany, with Metrical English Translations

Charles G. Leland

**English-Gipsy Songs**
*In Rommany, with Metrical English Translations*

ISBN/EAN: 9783337181369

Printed in Europe, USA, Canada, Australia, Japan

Cover: Foto ©Andreas Hilbeck / pixelio.de

More available books at **www.hansebooks.com**

# En Rommany

*WITH METRICAL ENGLISH TRANSLATIONS.*

BY

## CHARLES G. LELAND,
## PROFESSOR E. H. PALMER,
AND
## JANET TUCKEY.

LONDON:

TRÜBNER & CO., LUDGATE HILL.

1875.

PRINTED BY BALLANTYNE AND COMPANY
EDINBURGH AND LONDON

# Dedicated

## *ALFRED TENNYSON.*

# PREFACE.

—o—

WHEN writing "The English Gipsies and their Language," I was desirous of adding specimens of Rommany songs to the collection of proverbs and tales contained in the work, but could obtain none possessed of interest except as indifferent illustrations of the tongue. There is beyond doubt a great deal of singing in Rommany, but it is like that of American Indians, without form and void, wanting in metre and rhyme, and chanted to what only a very impressible disciple of Suggestive Art could recognise as a tune. I have often heard this kind of Gipsy ballad—indeed, it is not many days since an old dame, full of gratitude for a shilling which I had bestowed on her, having converted it into gin, and herself into its receptacle, followed me through the streets of Happy Hampton, singing my praises in Rommany. On another occasion, an old Gipsy told me that his sister, who had for some time announced it as her firm intention to die on the fifteenth day of the following month, had passed the previous evening in singing what she called her Death Song. All, however, that I could learn respecting it was, that it was a " werry lonesome " song, and " about a yard and a half long," as my informant indicated by extending his arms. It had "no tune in pertick'ler "—and, her brother seemed to think, no meaning in particular either. I am happy to say, by the way, that the prediction was not fulfilled, though the old woman's relations were quite persuaded that it would be so on the day appointed.

Not finding what I wanted, I had given up the intention of forming such a collection, when the perusal of a few excellent Rommany ballads by a friend who may fairly claim to be among the " deepest" of the deep in the language, as well as others by Professor Palmer and Miss Janet Tuckey, suggested to me the idea that poetry, impressed with true Gipsy spirit, and perfectly idiomatic, might be written and honestly classed as Rommany, even though not composed by dwellers in tents or caravans. The experiment was made, great care being taken to avoid anything like theatrical Gipsyism, or fanciful idealisation. With this constantly kept in mind, the writers have done their best to use simple language and to keep strictly to real English Rommany, both as regards words and expression. The difficulty of doing so was very great, it being often impossible to set forth new ideas correctly without exposing ourselves to the charge of making a new language, or creating, in the dilettanti spirit, an affected style. We have, I trust, done nothing towards forming a *lengua del Aficion*, or sham Gipsy, such as exists in Spain among sporting men, and is unintelligible to Gipsies. Not that I would regard this as an infallible test, for I have known Gipsies so ignorant that it was impossible without much explanation and many repetitions to make them understand the simplest English verse. But I venture to say that in this collection there is hardly one poem which, if read in a natural and prosaic manner, without dwelling on the rhymes or metre, will not be perfectly plain to any intelligent Gipsy ; indeed, I have amply satisfied myself of this by experiment.

There are many to whom writing ballads in a language possessing no literature, and almost unknown, save to a few vagabonds, will seem like a mere eccentric fancy. I would say in answer to this, that of late years Rommany has been a subject of great interest to the first philologists of Europe ; that in England it has for several centuries been a distinct dialect ; and that it is soft, musical, and easy to acquire. As it contains an extraordinary number of Hindi-Hindustani, Sanskrit, and Persian words, it can be of some assistance to persons who would study those languages. This may be inferred from the fact that an Indian military friend of mine once visited a Gipsy camp, and did his best to talk with its occupants through the medium of Hindustani. Afterwards one of the Gipsies informed me privately that my friend talked " werry bad Rommanis, but it *was* Rommanis—such as it was—and the gentleman was a Rommany rye."

The reader will find in this work, in addition to the poems, a Glossary, suggested by Mr Tennyson, and prepared by Professor E. H. Palmer; also a Rhyming Vocabulary by Miss Janet Tuckey. The Introduction and Notes appended to the poems are by myself.

CHARLES G. LELAND.

# CONTENTS.

—o—

# INTRODUCTION.

—o—

ENGLISH-GIPSY, as now spoken, presents the appearance of a language which was perhaps never fully developed, and is now in a state of rapid deterioration. At the end of the last century, J. C. C. Rüdiger discovered that Rommany, as the Gipsy tongue is properly called in all countries, was of Hindu origin, and this he announced in a work entitled, "Neuester Zuwachs der Sprachkunde," Halle, 1782. Later researches, among which I would specify those of Pott and Miklosich ("Ueber die Wanderungen der Zigeuner," &c., Wien, 1873), have more accurately determined that it belongs to the so-called "recent Indian" family, as a large proportion of its words are to be found in Hindustani or Persian, and its grammar resembles that of these languages. Yet its difference is on the whole so marked, that it must be ranked by itself as a language. Whether it was originally formed in

A

India, previous to the exodus of the Gipsy race, between the tenth and fourteenth centuries, or whether it assumed new grammatical forms during the wanderings of the people of the " dark blood," is not as yet known. The problem has excited great interest, and Miklosich, one of the most indefatigable of German philologists, is busily engaged in its solution. I would observe, with regard to the origin of Rommany, that my fellow-labourer, Professor E. H. Palmer, of Cambridge, has decided, on examining a vocabulary of more than four thousand English-Gipsy words collected by me, that nearly all of them, not of Greek or European origin, are Hindi or Persian, the Hindi greatly predominating. It is also to be remarked, that many Rommany words have an old Sanskrit character, and that, despite the mutilated, diluted, and impoverished state of this very singular language, there are reasons for believing that it contains the fragments or framework of some extremely ancient Aryan tongue, preserved from the earliest times among those wandering tribes, which have, since the days of the Vedas, maintained a privileged and separate existence, —as, for instance, the Dom.

Dr Miklosich has, with great ingenuity, pointed out from the fragments of Greek, Slavonic, and other tongues found in the different dialects of European Gipsies, the course of their travels, and conjectured the time they remained in different countries. It is a curious fact that the Anglo-Rommany, to judge from my own researches, contains far more Hindi and Persian words than any of the Continental dialects.

Until within fifty years, English Rommany was spoken with something like grammatical accuracy, and in that condition very much resembled the tongue as it now exists in Germany. It is not long since Dr Zupitza, of Vienna, discovered that the specimen of .so-called *Egyptian* in Andrew Borde's "Boke of the Introduction of Knowledge" (London, 1542) is really Rommany, and quite intelligible to most Gipsies. It is to be observed, that English Rommany contains only two or three French or German words—the former being all doubtful—and that, to judge from Borde's fragment, it had begun even in his time to Anglicise. There are still in England a few old Gipsies who pride themselves on preserving many grammatical forms and "deep" words, and many more who understand but do not use them. But the language is, on the whole, greatly changed, and to write it as it practically exists, without affecting archaisms on the one hand, or falling into mere jargon on the other, is a very difficult task.

It was accordingly no easy matter for my colleagues and myself to determine exactly the character of the

Rommany which we should adopt. We finally determined to write in the tongue as we familiarly understood it, and as we had found it—*i.e.*, in the current modern form; but retaining as much old Rommany as could be done with truth and ease.

Gipsies in one part of England understand many old words unknown to those in another, and very often an individual will recall some obsolete and curious term, apparently retained by him alone. I therefore trust that nobody will set it down to the discredit of these poems if he should find that, on reading them to the first basket-seller or fortune-teller, he or she should declare many words to be unintelligible, or call them "Dictionary Rommanis." I am not apprehensive that the more intelligent Gipsies will fail to understand the work.

The reader desirous of further information on the subject of this language may consult the "Romano Lavo Lil" of George Borrow (London, John Murray, 1874), and the excellent book on the English-Gipsy language by Dr Bath C. Smart (London, Asher & Co., 1875), in which the tongue is given in the so-called deep or archaic form.

C. G. L.

———0———

KÉRRI mūllo yol a lélled
  Lāki's kūramengro rom;
Pāli o' ye tánya jelled,
  Chivved les trūppo pré the dróm.
    But odoi yoi beshed alay,
      Sim a mūllo, 'pré the pūv
    Keker shelled or hatched apré,
    Kek'nai kairdas lāki rúvv.

Sār o' lākis jūvas dick
  Rākkerin yoi sasti rúvv;
Else yoi'll mūller 'dré ye chick,
  Mūller 'doi apré ye pūv.
    But odoi yoi beshed alay, &c.

Pūkk'das lén a míshto pen:
  " Yúv sos a būt kūshto mūsh,
Kairin pálor táchipen,
  Kairin górgio geeror dúsh."
    But odoi yoi beshed alay, &c.

Sims a chór fon lākis tán
  Būt shūkár a jūva wélled ;
Pirried kéti mūllo án,
  O diklo 'vrī les' mūi lelled.
    But odoi yoi beshed alay, &c.

Hatched apró a pūri dye,
  Lāk's chávo pré her chóng she chívs :
Sims a brishin róvel yoi :
  " Tūkey kāmmaben, mi jivs ! "

        *Translated by* E. H. PALMER.

# HOME THEY BROUGHT HER WARRIOR DEAD.

—o—

HOME they brought her warrior dead :
   She nor swooned nor uttered cry :
All her maidens watching said—
   " She must weep or she will die."

Then they praised him, soft and low,
   Called him worthy to be loved,
Truest friend and noblest foe ;
   Yet she neither spoke nor moved,

Stole a maiden from her place,
   Lightly to the warrior stept,
Took the face-cloth from his face ;
   Yet she neither moved nor wept.

Rose a nurse of ninety years,
   Set his child upon her knee—
Like summer tempests came her tears :
   " Sweet, my child, I live for thee."

ALFRED TENNYSON.

——o——

" Dordi, mi pal—ko jívela
    Adré o boro kér adoi ? "
" Tu dínnelo chal, i krállissa !—
    Mā pen tu's kékker shūned o' yoi !

" I kūshti rāni—āvali :
    Yoi kāmela o chóro mūsh,
Te yói's sā sīg 'dré lākis zī
    For sār i kāli fókis dūsh.

" *Sā mandy sosti jin o' lis ?*
    Del kán : adré o wāver besh
Mándy te mīri romani
    Sos pīrryin' pāsh o krállis' wésh.

" Mándy te mīri rōmani
    Sos jūllin kéti gáv acai ;
Te mōro chávos, kétteni,
    Beshed pré o dūmo o' ye gry.

" ' Oh, hatch a kūsi, deari rom,'
Mi poori jūva pènela;
' Mā jāl andūro—kínlo shom !—
Kair mōro bitti tan kennā.'

" Sos yeck wenésto dívvus, pal :
O pūv sos pāno sārapré ;
O bávol pūdered fon shimál ;
O yiv pelled súrrelo tuléy.

" Sos dush ta hatch a tan adói
Adré adóvo shíllopen :
Ko'll sikker mèngy cávacoi—
Sossi Midúvel kairs o wén ?

" I chávor rūdered pré a lay
Ta latcher kóshter tull' o yiv,
Te mándy kaired o yāg apré—
Sos dūsheri ta kair lis jív.

" Hūkki, tu jins, amándi lelled
Trin chávos, sārjā bóckeli :
Adré adóvo rātti welled,
Dūi wāver tíknor, kétteni.

" Ovāvo dívvus vias a mūsh—
Sos i krallíssas yāgengro ;
' Mā hatch kekūmi 'dre o wesh !'
Yuv pūkked améngy, húnnalo.

"Yeck o' mi chávos shelled avrī:
    'Rye, dick a wóngish 'drĕ o tan—
Dick yéckora, sā rínkeni
    I dūi névvi tíknor shán!'

"Yuv chívdas shèrro pāsh adrè:
    Ah, sos būt dūkkeri ta dick
I jūva, shillerin' dóvalay,
    I tíknor, beeno 'prĕ o chick.

"Sos kāmmoben 'drĕ lester yāk:
    'Dūi, dūi!' péndas yuv ajā;
Adóvo sī too būti bāk        ·
    For túte—tácho, mīro bā?'

"An' sā yuv pírried sig adróm,
    'Dūi, dūi!' sos yúvs lástus lav.
Pal, shūn kennā: 'drĕ dóvo shám
    Díckdum a bitti wárdo av.

"O yāgengro sos tūllin lis;
    'Rom, ávacai!' yuv pūkked ajā,
Sī chúmmeny kūshto, dick a lis,
    Sār bítchered fón i krállissā.

"'Yoi's shūned o' tīro dūkkerben—
    I dūi tiknor chívved acai;
Acóvo's lākis délaben
    For tiri chávor te i dye.'

" Sos būti 'dré o wárdo, pal :
　　Dūi bōro cóppas—āvali !—
　Hābben, yeck wálin lūllo mol—
　　Miduvelést' i Rānis zī !

" Pāsh rínkeni heezis—shūn kennā—
　　Sos būti tátti hōvalos ;
　Yoi tivdas len—i krállissā—
　　I rāni pré i Gorgios !

" I bōro chávos, sār i trin,
　　Rivved dóvo hōvalos apré :
　Yúl dicked sā kūshto, prásterin
　　Sā rínkeni chúkkered, pré a lay.

" Tácho, shan bárvelo Górgios,
　　Būti, adré acóvo tem,
　Ko'd kām ta sikker hōvalos
　　Tivved pā i Rānis noko fem.

" Mi kāmli jūva ásti mér
　　Tal' mōro Rānis délaben :
　Tácho, mi kāmava ta kair
　　Vārisso, lākis kāmmoben.

" If yoi kāmel'a mūsh ta kūr,
　　Shom sār acai ! Pal áv ajā—
　Mūkks pī a tás o' levinor
　　For kām o' moro krállissa !"

Janet Tuckey.

—o—

" Look, brother—tell me if you know
      Who lives in that big castle there ? "
" The Queen, you stupid !   Now don't go
      A-sayin' you've ne'er heard of *her.*

" For she's a right good lady—yes,
      She loves the poor, ay, that she do !
And she can feel for the distress
      Of wandering folk like me and you.

" *And how do I know that ?*   Well, hark :
      One day last year my wife and me
Were travelling by Windsor Park—
      Those trees out yonder, do you see ?

" My wife and me were going along
      Towards Windsor—just afore you there—
The children, all together, clung
      Upon the back of our old mare.

" But my poor girl said : ' Stop a bit
    And let me rest, O husband dear !
I can't go further, I'm not fit ;
    Just set our little tent up here.'

" That was a wintry day, my lad !
    One whiteness over all the place ;
The bitter north-wind blew like mad ;
    The snow came stinging in one's face.

" I tell you 'twas no easy task
    In all that cold to pitch a tent ;
And here's a thing I'd like to ask—
    Why is the cruel winter sent ?

" Under the snow the children sought,
    And found some sticks, just four or five :
I made a fire of what they brought ;
    'Twas hard to keep the flame alive.

" Already, do you mind, we had
    Three sons—enough to manage for :
Well, on that very night, my lad,
    The wife had twins—ay, two boys more !

" The morning after came a gent—
    The Queen's head-gamekeeper, I knew :
Said he : ' How dare you stick your tent
    Up here, you lazy Gipsy, you ?'

" One of my little chaps called out :
   ' Sir, won't you look a bit in there,
And see the babies mother's got ?—
   Such pretty little things they are ! '

" He put his head just half-way in :
   Ah, 'twas a cheerless sight he found—
My wife, poor dear, a-shiverin',—
   The babies, born upon the ground.

" He looked with pity in his eyes :
   ' Twins, twins !' he cried—' why there you got
Rather too much of a surprise,
   My poor old fellow, did you not ? '

" And when he turned and left us soon,
   ' Twins, twins !' again I heard him say.
Now listen : that same afternoon
   A little light-cart came our way.

" The gamekeeper was driving it :
   ' Come on,' he cried, ' you've never seen
A cart-load such as this, I bet—
   And it's a present from the Queen.'

" ' She's heard what troubles you have had—
   Your two poor babies, born in there,

And of your wife who's lyin' so bad,
　　So she has sent these things for her.'

" Well, there was plenty in that cart :
　　A pair of blankets for my wife,
Food, and a bottle full of port ;—
　　God bless that Lady all her life !

" There were some clothes too, and between
　　Lay children's woollen stockings, those
She'd knitted—she herself—the Queen,
　　The Lady of the Gorgios !

" The biggest children, all the three,
　　Put each a pair of stockings on ;
They looked as pretty as could be,
　　Well shod, and trotting up and down.

" Thought I : there's many a Gorgio—
　　Rich lords and ladies in the land,
Who'd be uncommon proud to show
　　Socks knitted by the Queen's own hand.

" But for that Lady I'd have had
　　To see my wife die over there ;
You needn't wonder, need you, lad,
　　That I'd do anything for her.

" So if she wants a man to box,
   I'll fight her battles, never fear !—
   'Twas dry work talking of them socks—
   Let's drink the Queen's good health in beer."

JANET TUCKEY.

The editor has often heard the incident here narrated from an old Gipsy, well known in Windsor.

# "JĀL ANI!"

——o——

PĀSH o 'the bor, kai stékka' shán,
  Pāsh o the rūkk' sar póggadi ;
Beshdom kan pīrdos chivved a tan
  Te shūnd'em rākker Rómmany.

Ye bítti chávi' jian avrī
  To lel a bitt' o kosht for len ;
I pūri Liz,—būt húnnalī—
  Rākkerdas bitti tíknos pen.

Léssi a nísseri cóvva, kún
  O tānopen sims ye pūreni ;
Te bórodīr paiáss to shūn
  Ye tíknor rākkeran Rómmany.

Te sā i graior jian to chār,
  Te sā the yāg sos kérelo ;
Avrī o drúm, te pāl' the bor,
  Vas mōro gáv-mūsh, húnnalo.

B

"Jā vrī! yúv rākker's as he wélled :
    "Or mándy 'll klisin tūte, sār :"—
"Kéress tu 'dúlla," Lizzie shélled,
    "Star mándy 'dré o kítchemā."

"Jūl án !" pens o gavéngero,
    "Tūte's kek sīg to hátch acói ! "
"Tácho ;" pens Petuléngero
    "Kék sīg to jív—'kai or odói !"

Sā sār ye pīredor jālled án,
    Āwer sigán sos kūshti sā ;
'Dré wāver drum len kairdé tan
    I 'kávī būllerin ajā.

Te shūnin lénders sávvyins,
    Pendum : sā kūshto cóvva sī
For būti geeros mandy jins,
    Te sásti jā, sā sīg avrī.

Avrī o Lundraméscro jiv,
    Kairin an' rākkerin dínnalo,
Avrī the kérya, vrī the chiv,
    Kai yúl sūrjá shán húnnalo.

Húnn'lo o tátto kairoben,
    Húnn'lo o sār that's rínkení ;

Húnn'lo o kūshto kāmmābcn
Or kairin sīg sārja to be.

O, sos a boro, kūshto pem
To shūn a mūllo rākker : " Mān !"
Yeck gav-mūsh 'dré Midúvels tem,
Sav' péu'lla : " Tūl your chiv! jāl an !"

CHARLES G. LELAND.

——o——

By the ragged hedge and straggling fence,
    Beneath the broken willow-tree,
I sat, while Gipsies pitched their tents
    Around, and chaffed in Rommany.

The children, who could hardly walk,
    Were sent to pick a bit of wood ;
Old Liz, so fierce in all her talk,
    Spoke as a little infant should.

Ah ! when old age grows young again—
    And such old age—it's strange to see ;
And stranger still to think there should
    Be baby-talk in Rommany.

But, as the horses went to graze,
    And as the fire began to burn,
Out of the lane, among the strays,
    Came our Inspector, grim and stern.

" You know that this won't do," he cried.
   " Be off, or I shall lock you up ! "
" If you do that," old Liz replied,
   " Please lock me in a cookin' shop."

" Pack and be out of this forthwith !
   You know you have no business here ! "
" No ; we hain't got," said Samuel Smith,
   " No business to be Anywhere."

So wearily they went away,
   Yet soon were camped in t'other lane,
And soon they laughed as wild and gay,
   And soon the kettle boiled again.

And as they settled down below,
   I could but think upon the bliss
'Twould be to many men I know
   To move as lightly " out of this : "—

Out of this life of morning calls,
   And weary work, and wasted breath ;
These prison cells of pictured walls,
   Where they are always " bored to death."

Bored by all kinds of cleverness,
   Bored by the beautiful and fair ;
By love, and joy, and tenderness ;
   Or, if not bored, pretend they are.

Oh, what a blessing it would be
    To hear some angel cry, " Be gone ! "
Some heavenly Inspector C.,
    Who'd say, " Now none of this—Move on ! "

                            CHARLES G. LELAND.


It is perhaps almost needless to say that this is a sketch from life.   I recall, however, that it was not a Smith, but one of the Matthews, who remarked to the Inspector that " We have no right to be anywhere."   Old Liz is the same Rommany who told me that she was sure the Shah was one of " the people."

# I KÉRÉNGRI.

——o——

Tu pendas mengy " Sārishan ? "
De wāver dívvus, pal, acai
Adrè acóvva werry tan.
Pens mándy " So's adóvo rye ? "

" So's sikkered lis to be sā flick,"
I pens, " at rākkerin Rommany ? "—
Kek búti chals does mandy dick
For mándy's a kéréngeri.

Ah, rye ! a gávs a wáfro tan ;
Shom Rómmani, *I* kāms ye drom !
Āvo ! fon *tute* " sārishan ? "
And gorgio's jib fon nóko rom !

E. H. PALMER.

# THE HOUSE-DWELLER.

YOU passed me by this werry way,
An' "*Sarishan ?*" you said to me.
I've often wondered, since that day,
What sort of person you might be ?

Says I, "Them's Gipsy words he spoke,
But where could he ha' learnt, and how ?"—
I don't see much o' Romm'ny folk,
I'm livin' in a house, sir, now.

I hate this sort o' life, I do !
I'm Rommany, and want to roam.—
Just fancy ! "*sarishan ?*" from *you*,
And only English talk at home !

E. H. PALMER.

This poem is true to life in every line, as it was expressed
to the writer by a Gipsy woman who had left off wandering.
The word *pal* or brother is very characteristic. Any gentleman who addresses the humblest Gipsy in Rommany must
expect to be called pal, not disrespectfully, but because it is
incident to the language. It is *prala* in other countries.

# O RÓMMANI PÓSSERBEN ADRÉ O PŪRO CHĪRUS.

———o———

A tíkno, rẏa?—Àvali, yéckorus amándi lelled yeck,
A bítti chávi, sā rínkeni sā tūte kāmessa ta dick ;
Kána yoi vias arātti adré mōro pūro tán,
Sos pensi o dūd o' the sāla a-pūkkerin Sārishán.

Mīri jūva sos būt míshto, te sā lākis tikno te yoi
Sos béshin túller i rūkkor te másker i rūzhior adoi,
Mi látcherdum yeck mūiéngri man dicked dré a
    būddika, rye,
I fóki péndás sos Midúvel a-béshin pāsh lésker dye.

I mýla, i jūva, te mándy jássede kéttenes 'pré o drom—
'Sār i chávi 'dré yeck trusháro—oh, shomas a bāktolo
    Rom !
Te kána i rātti sos wéllin, sār dūr fon i gávior,
Amándi hatched mōro tan pāsh o tátto rikk o' the bor.

Pāsh o yāg, ríkkorus o tan, mendūi béshdum alay,
Te rākkered' ajā kún i chávi sos sútto pūkeno adré,
Sā men sósti síkker lāki ta kil 'dré i wellgorós,
Te lel būt adústa wóngur a-dūkkerin Górgios.

Awer, 'dré o rínkeno chīrus, te pāli o bōro wen,
Moro déari kūmeli chávi lelled o wáfro náflopen ;
Lākis tāni pīrror sos shíllo, sār shilleri sims i yiv,
Āwer lākis chámyor lūlldé, pensi rūzhior másker o
     giv.

Miri jūva pūkkerdas mándy : "Rom, hatch apré te jā
Kéti gav, te māng o drabéngro ta kíster acai kennā."
Mi lelldum drabéngro, āwer kún amándi welled ketteni,
Mi dickdum yuv násti kair chīchī—i chávi sos sóved avrī.

Mi jūva rovélla būti, āwer mandy péndum kek lav,
Till apré o wāver pāsh-dívvus a mūsh avéll' fon o gav ;
Lester rūderpen síkkeras mándy yuv sos a bōro rashái :
Yuv kāmed to rākker būt cóvvas ké méngy te mīri chi.

Yúv rākkered, te mándy shūndom, till lástus yuv
     pūkker's ajā :
"Tute'll kām to chiv tiri chávi 'dré o kángry pūv kennā ?
Sī a kūshto cóvva to hatch 'dré i lock o' Midúvel's
     kér"——
"Kékker, kekker, rýa!" mi shélldum, "mi'd kām
     siggadīro to mer."

" Sí adóvo a tácho cóvva, mi rya, so tūte pen,
O' ye fóki hátchin apré 'dré o bōro shūnaben,
Miri chávi'd mér apopli, yoi'd lel sā trásheni,
If yoi díckdas a tan o' Górgios pāsh lākis kōkeri.

" I tāni sósti sov kai i kāmeli rūzhior shán—
Kai i táchi Rommani cháls avéllan to hatch o tan—
Kai, sār o tátto dívvus i pīrri chíriclos pūkk,
Te o rūkestamengro hóckers, lellin pīvlor apré o rūkk."

Mi ghiom adré o wésh, te mi kaírdum a hev shūkár;
Yeck bóro rínkeno rūkk sos mi dearis shérro-bar :
Tuller būti rūzhior yoi béshela pūkeno adré—
Āwer mándy penáva, mi rýe, yoi'll kékker hūshti apré !

JANET TUCKEY.

——o——

A BABY, sir? surely, yes! a long while since we had one,
A little daughter, as pretty as e'er you set eyes upon;
She came to our poor old tent in the darkest hour of the
    night,
And, I tell you, it seemed as if day'd broke sudden, to
    cheer us with light.

My wife was wonderful glad; and when she and that
    baby of ours
Were sitting together, sir, under trees, in the midst of
    flowers,
I used to remember a picture I'd seen in a shop long ago;—
'Twas the Lord by His mother's side—at least the folk
    there told me so.

We'd travel along all day, the donkey, myself, and my wife,
With the baby in one of the panniers—ah! that was a
    real good life!
And when the evening came on, in the quietest spot we
    could find,
We'd pitch our tent by the hedge, on the opposite side
    from the wind.

Near the fire, just close to the tent, my wife and myself
    would sit,
And talk for a while of the child, who was sleeping
    inside of it :
How careful we'd bring her up to dance at the fairs
    some day,
And tell Gorgios' fortunes, so as to charm their money
    away.

But just as the winter passed, and the beautiful spring-
    dawn smiled,
A fever went through the land, and she took it—our
    only child !
Cold, ay, colder than snow was the touch of her poor
    little feet,
But her cheeks were burning red, like the poppies among
    the wheat.

Said her mother to me at night : " Rise quickly, O hus-
    band dear—
Quickly, and run to the town, and fetch us the doctor
    here."
I went, and I fetched him back, but as soon as I looked
    at the bed,
I knew that he'd come too late, for my little daughter
    was dead !

My wife cried bitter, but I could only sit stupidly
    down,
And I hadn't a word, till next day a gentleman came
    from the town—
A preaching gentleman, sir,—I know it by his clothes,
    d'ye see—
And he set himself down by my side, and preached to
    my wife and me.

He talked, and we let him talk, and never answered a
    word,
Till he said, " You'll be wanting to bury your baby in
    our churchyard ?
In the shadow of God's own house 'tis a blessed thing
    to lie "——
But " Never, never ! " I cried ; " no, sir, I would sooner
    die ! "

Said I : " If it's really true, certain and true, what you
    say,
That the folk will rise from their graves on the Lord's
    great judgment-day,
Why, if *my* child was to wake with a crowd of Gorgios
    in sight,
She'd feel so strange, I believe she'd die over again with
    fright.

" My little darling must sleep where the beautiful flowers
   grow ;
Where the squirrel gathers his nuts, leaping merrily to
   and fro ;
Where the Gipsies may pitch their tent at the closing
   of summer eves,
And birds through the summer days may sing under
   shadowing leaves."

So I went and I dug a grave in the quietest part of the
   wood,
Where a tree, grown higher than the rest, for my baby's
   headstone stood ;
And there, under many flowers, she is lying so calm and
   still ;
But, sir, as for rising again, why, I don't think she ever
   will.

JANET TUCKEY.

In the old times, or till within fifty years, the Gipsies buried
their dead in lonely and remote places ; but now they mani-
fest great anxiety to secure Christian burial, and incur con-
siderable expense in funerals. The same change has taken
place with regard to their indifference to a future state, or
a disbelief in it ; their irreligion having been in reality
ignorance of and hostility to all the rules and institutions
of civilisation. The younger Gipsies of the better class would
now generally be offended if any doubt of their Christianity

were expressed. But that some relics of the " creed outworn," or, rather, of ancient custom, still linger in the mind of the modern Gipsy, may be inferred from the fact that very recently, and since the foregoing ballad was written, a young Rommany girl of superior attainments protested that she would not like to be buried in a churchyard, but rather in some wild place, where her Gipsy kinsfolk would come and pitch their tents.

J. T.

# O TÁCHO ROM.

Oh, mándy's yéck o' lénder as jāl apré the drom,
A tácho Petuléngro an' a kūshto pūro Rom.
Miro kāko sī a Chilcott, mīri dya sī a Lee,
Awer mán shóm ferridīro an' a kālo Rómmany.
  An' a tácho Rommany,
   'Pré mī mórtchi, 'dré mī zī.
Who-op ! Dick adré mī yākkor, an pūkker : "Avali !"

Mándy jāls to ye welgóras, mándy's sārasār adói ;
Yéck dívvus longo-dūro, te wāver kāvacói :
Yéck dívvus kūshti rūdered, díckin sims a bóro rye,
Denn' sā a māngermēngro, a-tūlin of yer gry.
  " Just a rūpp'ni bitto, rye,
   For a-tūlin of yer gry !"
Who-op ! mándy jins arātti to kíster off a gry !

When I'm chínnin o' the péggor, mándy dicks sā pūkkeno,
Tūte'd pen dóv' Petuléngro sī a tácho váccasho ;
But I'm flícknor o' my wástors nor any wāver Rom,
An' can mūller any geero as jāls apré the drom.
  At kūrin, mándy shóm
   Sīg to bónger, sīg to slom ;
Oh, at déllin or at kéllin I'm a táchodīro Rom.

            c

Sārishán, mi gūdli rāni ; sārishán, mi kūshto rye !
Mándy's jūva'll lel your wóngur kán yói avéll' akái.
Tūte'll kām to del la chúmmeny to pī your kāmmoben,
So I'll hátcher pūl' the kúnsus while she pens your
    dūkkerin.

Oh ! there'll be a pūkkerin,
  An' a bōro rākkerin,

Then I'll pén you kūshti rātti till I wéll this dróm again.

CHARLES G. LELAND.

# THE REAL GIPSY.

———o———

Oh ! I'm a jolly Gipsy, and I roam the country round ;
I'm a real Petulengro as can anywhere be found :
My uncle is a Chilcott, my mother is a Lee,
But I'm the best of all of 'em, and real Rommany.
                    A real Rommany
                    From head to foot I be.
Who-op ! look into my peepers if a Gipsy you would see !


I go to fairs and races, there I'm always to be found ;
One day across the country, then back upon the ground :
One day I'm dressed up swelly, like the gentleman of
        course,
Then the next I come the beggar, a holdin' of yer
        horse.
                    " Just a threepence, sir.   All right !
                    For I held him jolly tight."
Who-op ! I'm the boy as knows the way to run a horse
        —by night !

When a cuttin' of my skewers, so peaceable I am,
You'd say, " That Petulengro is the pattern of a lamb!"
But I'm handy with my maulies, as I many a time have
　　showed,
An' can do for any traveller as goes upon the road.
　　　　Oh ! at fightin' I'm at home,
　　　　Quick to dodge an' quick to come ;
For at hittin' or at shyin' I'm an out-an'-outer Rom !

How *are* you, my sweet lady ? how are *you*, my lord ?
　　I say :
My wife'll take your money when she comes along this
　　way.
You'll want to give her something—just to keep away
　　the cold—
So I'll step round the corner while your fortune's bein'
　　told.
　　　　Then there'll be a patterin',
　　　　An' an awful chatterin' !
So I bid you all good evenin' till I come this way again.

　　　　　　　　　　　CHARLES G. LELAND.

# O TÓVER.

———o———

Wanty had chívved a bítti tán,
Kék dūr fon Lilengrésky gáv ;
Te díckdas a mī and a pāsh o' ran',
A bōro'in pāsh o' the dūiyav.
Āwer as yuv sā sīg and flick
A wásta-pord o' de ránya chíns,
Sávo should well adói an' dick,
But o mūsh as lélled de tan, you jins ?
    Āvalí, wáfro, wáfro sī !
    Te wáfro bāk for de Rómmani chals.
    For de Górgiko rye has wélled acái,
    An' Wanty has náshered his tóver, pals !

Adóvo sús dúsh for the mūsh, he wélled
Kérri apópli with póggado zī ;—
Kek ránya kéti de tánya lélled,
Te yúv's rínkení tóver jālled avrī.
"Oh ! mándy wouldn't ha' lélled a bár,
Nor dūi—nor yet if yer délled mi trin

For adóva tóver ; o' tóvers sār
Adóva sús kūshtiest ta chín.
    Āvalí, wáfro, wáfro sī ! &c.

"Oh ! deari jūva ! oh ! pūri dye !
Oh, pálor and chálor ! and Rómni and Rom !
Oh ! práster avrī kéti Górgiko rye,
An pen sār tūkeno mándy shom,
Te mándy'll kek-kekkūmi jā
A chórin' cóvvas at lésker tan,
Kek-kūmi apópli káir ajā,
Kek-kūmi apópli chín a ran.
    Āvali, wáfro, wáfro sī !" &c.

Oh ! lésker pal and léskri pén,
Te lésker dádas and léskri dye,
Shan jāllin ta māng de shūnaben
O' de bōro, bárvelo, Górgiko rye.
"Oh ! lél the tan talé o bor
Te sār i cóvvas so shán adré ;
Oh ! lél de wárdo, o gry te sār,
Āwer dél de tóver—dél lis opré !"
    Āvali, kūshto, kūshto sī !
    Oh ! kūshto bāk for de Rommany chals.
    For the Górgiko rye has jālled avrī,
    An' Wanty has latchered his tóver, pals !

                E. H. PALMER.

## THE HATCHET.

——o——

WANTY had pitched his little tent
Near Cambridge in the meadows wide,
When he saw an osier-bed that went
A mile along the river-side.
But as he cut so fast and free
The osiers with a nimble hand,
Whoever should he chance to see,
But the gentleman who owned the land.
    Oh, dear! we ain't in luck to-day!
    Oh! it's bad, bad luck for the Gipsy lad:
    For the farmer's come and he's taken away
    The beautiful axe that Wanty had.

Oh! that was bad for the lad: he went
Home broken-hearted and all alone;
Never took an osier back to the tent,
An' his beautiful axe was lost and gone.
Says he, " I wouldn't ha' taken a pound,
Nor two—nor yet if yer giv me three,

For that axe; in all the country round
There was none like that for fellin' a tree.
Oh, dear! we ain't in luck to-day, &c.

" Oh! run dear wife, and mother too,
And brother and sister, and lass and lad ;
Oh! run away to the farmer, do!
Say I'm so sorry I'm almost mad.
I'll never—never go there no more
A stealin' anythin' off his land ;
And I'll never do like I've done before,
Nor touch an osier with this 'ere hand.
Oh, dear! we ain't in luck to-day!" &c.

Off went his sister, off went his mate,
Off went his father, and mother too,
To beg for pardon and make it straight
With that good, kind farmer so well to do.
" Oh! take away the tent we've pitched,
The camp from top to bottom sack!
Oh! take the van and the horse that's hitched
To the shafts—but give us the hatchet back."
Hooray! hooray! well done, I say!
Good luck for the Gipsies, instead o' bad ;
The farmin' gent has gone away,
And given the hatchet back, my lad!
E. H. PALMER.

The story of Wanty is strictly true, with the exception of
a change of name and place.  The Gipsy was engaged with a
friend in getting wood from a hedge when they were surprised
by the farmer, who punished them in the manner described.
I was in the camp by the river when the two unfortunates
returned, and were obliged to give an account of the loss to a
third Gipsy who had lent them the hatchet.  I have heard
"wales" and outcries in my life, but nothing like what
occurred on this occasion.  The reader who would form an
idea of the scene may, however, find something resembling it
in the Prologue to the Fourth Book of Rabelais, where the
small country gentlemen bewail their loss of the same instru-
ment.  "Verily, they cried out, and brayed, and prayed, and
bawled, and invoked Jupiter: My hatchet! my *hatchet!*
Jupiter, my hatchet! . . . The air round about rung again
with the cries and howlings of these rascally losers of hatchets."
The solemn tone with which the owner, looking out from the
window of his van, pronounced an oration over the missing
article, thereby tacitly wounding the feelings of the losers,
was a study for an actor.  "I wouldn't a' taken four bob for
that hatchet," he said ; "and I wouldn't a' taken five, nor six :
I wouldn't a' taken *eight*—nor a pound—and (rising to a
climax)—I wouldn't a' taken NO money for it.  I've had it
with me in all my travels—it was the best hatchet on the road
or anywhere.  It an't more'n a week since I gave a man a
shillin for sharpenin of it."  Here the loser, in accents of con-
trition, exclaimed : "Nobody could a' done more than I did
to get it back.  I *most* went down on my knees for it—and
by an' by, when I goes to beg him again, I *will*.  And I never
will be such a fool as to go a chorin kosh (stealing wood)
out of any man's hedge—by daylight—agin—never no more."
He did, presently, reinforced by his family, make an appeal
which was successful, and the axe was returned to him.

—o—

Mī ghíom adūro dyéscri tán,
Te o Górgio vias to látcher mán :
Sos sélno pátrinor 'pré o shock ;
Sos kūshto táller i rūkkor lock ;
Yūv díckdas a méngy sā kāmeli—
Kek jindas mī shómas Rómmani.

O kām péshed rínkeno 'pré mendūi ;
Yúv díckdas 'dré mīro kālo mūi,
Mīrī kāli yākkor, mī kālo fem :
Yúv péndas : "Avéss' fon a wāver tem—
Fon a tátto tem būti-dūr avrī ?"
Kékker pūkkdom mī shómas Rómmani.

"Avéss' sār mándy !" yúv mānged ajā :
Man mūkkerdom dádas te dye te sā ;
Kekkūmi ghiom kéti tan tūlák,
To pūkker i pályor kūshto bāk.
Yúv rúmmerdas mándy sā tácheni,
Āwer kékker jínned shómas Rómmani.

Jiváv' 'drín o rínkeno kér kennā,
Āwer shom būt trásheni sārasā :
Yeck dívvus mī rye shūnélla, shyán,
Léskri chi sos beeno adrín a tán ;
Te i fóki 'vel pūkker sā vássavi—
"Dick o mūsh so rúmmered a Rómmani !"

Sī shūnélla ke man shom kek Górgio,
Yúv te vel sā láj lester kókero,
Yúv'll kām to gáver adrín o kér—
Oh, kāmlo rom, mándy'd sīgger mér !
Mandy'd sīgger jāl sārasār avrī
Ténna kair tūt' láj ap i Rómmani.

Yói ghias sā sīg kéti doéyav ;
Yói pūkkdas yéckli o rýas náv ;
Yói hátchdas adói pāsh o pánni kin,
Te wūsserdas kókeri sīg adrín :
"Pa tīro kāmmoben—āvali—
Merāva kennā, tīri Rómmani.

JANET TUCKEY.

# GIPSY DEATH FOR LOVE.

I WANDERED far from my mother's tent;
Alone through the shade of the woods I went :
Where leaves grew greenest, where trees were high,
We met in the shadow, my love and I.
So kindly and fondly he gazed at me—
But he did not know I was Rommani.

He led me out where the sun shone down,
He looked at my face that was Gipsy-brown ;
He looked in my eyes, and he took my hand ;
He said, "You come from a distant land—
From a warmer country across the sea ?"
I never told I was Rommani.

"Come, love !" he said.   When I heard him call,
I left my mother and home and all :
I never turned to the tent again,
To bid goodbye to the Gipsy men.
My Gorgio married me faithfully,
But he never knew I was Rommani.

And now I live like a lady here,
But I'm never safe from a thought of fear :
They'll tell my husband some day, with scorn,
Of the Gipsy tent where his wife was born ;
And the folk will cry when he passes, " See
The man that married a Rommani ! "

If he knew me for one of the Gipsy race,
He could never look Gorgios in the face,
He'd be glad to hide in the house all day :
O husband ! I'd sooner go far away,
And death would be easier far to me
Than seeing you ashamed of your Rommani.

She rose, and soon to the stream she came ;
But once she whispered her husband's name :
She stood awhile by the water-side,
Then cast herself in the flowing tide.
" 'Tis for love of you, O dear heart ! " said she;
" Now you'll never be shamed by the Rommani."

JANET TUCKEY.

I believe that the story given in this poem is quite true.
Alice Cooper told me of a Gipsy girl who, having married a
respectable Englishman, committed suicide, the reason being
that she had kept her Rommany origin a secret, and was afraid,

if it were found out, her husband would be ashamed of her. Alice was quite sure that no fear of his anger caused her to drown herself. "She was alaj her rye would latcher she was Rommany"—"She was ashamed her gentleman-husband would find that she was Gipsy," was the simple explanation of the sad event.

In Weybridge Churchyard, within a mile from the place where I heard this, there is a tombstone placed over the grave of another Gipsy girl named Roland, who drowned herself for love. It may be easily seen from the road, as it lies just by the wall.

## O FOTOGRAFÉNGRO.

—o—

" Mīro rýa," pendas o Rómmani,
    " 'S is tīro prettygraph lélled ?
Tu sósti díckavit—āvali—
    'T dívvus mī nóko was délled.

" The mūsh as kair'd o' mī landskip
    Pátsered to kéravit bōro.
Péndom mándy, ' Sátcho—if't isn't tácho,
    Tu násti lellav a hórro.'

" Lis rígdom adré mīro shérro ajū,
    That apré mīro hóvalo
Shán tácho desh-dūi cráfnies, bā,
    Te yéck cráfni sos násherdo.

" An' kána t' landskip sos léllo, aye,
    It kaired mán' sīg o' mī zī,
For sūr o' them cráfnies shánas adói,
    'Cept the yéck as sos pélled avrī.

" So penāva 'dúl' mūsh sī a tácheno mūsh
  As ever pīrried a pūv :
Kána Rommanis kām mūićngerīs,
  Bitchāva len sār to yúv."

CHARLES G. LELAND.

# THE PHOTOGRAPHER.

———o———

" My master," said the Gipsy man,
    " Is your prettygraph in your book ?
You ought to have seen it when mine was drawn,
    So that not a thing was mistook.

" The fellow who took my landscape perfessed
    He'd make it the best in town ;
' Wery well,' says I, ' if you don't, I'm blessed
    If I gives you a single brown ! '

" Now, I says to myself, ' On my leather tights
    A dozen of buttons is sewn :
A dozen he ought to give by rights,
    Hexceptin' the one as is gone.'

" But when that landskip was done so fair,
    I tell you, it took me down ;
For every one o' them buttons was there,
    Hexceptin' the one as was gone.

" So I 'olds that chap is a *hon*orable chap,
    As hever on earth I see ;
An when any one wants a prettygraph done,
    I sends 'em along to he."

                              CHARLES G. LELAND.

The incident embodied in this song was narrated to me in
all seriousness by a Gipsy; and were it not for the rhyme and
metre, I might say that it is here given almost in his words,
"prettygraph" and "landskip" being used, under the impression that they were quite correct.

# ROMMANY GILLI.

———0———

" KAI sos tu, rínkeno chávo, kai ? "
" Apré at ye well-góro, pals ;
    An' I hóckered a gry,
    An' I chóred a rye,
An' sār for ye kām o' ye Rómmany cháls ! "


" Kai sos tu, rínkeni jūva, kai ? "
" Apré at ye bōro gáv, my pals ;
    An' I dūkkered a rāni,
    An' chóred a kāni,
An' sār for ye kām o' ye Rómmany cháls ! "


" Kai sos tu o dívvus, pūri dye ? "
" Apré at ye farmin' kér, my pals ;
    And kālico sāla
    I drábbed a būlo,
An' sār for ye kām o' ye Rómmany cháls ! "

" Kai shán tu, bóshoméngro, kai ?"
" Oh, mándy shom sār akái, mī pals :
    An' mándy'll kíll,
    An' ye jūva'll gíll,
An' sār for ye kām o' ye Rómmany cháls ! "

E. H. PALMER.

# A GIPSY SONG.

———o———

"OH, where have you been, my bonny lad?"
"Oh, I have been up at the fair, my boys,
    With a hack to sell,
    And I cheated a swell,
And all for the love of the Gipsy boys!"

"Oh, where have you been, my pretty maid?"
"Oh, I have been up at the town, my boys;
    And a fortune I've told,
    And this chicken behold,
Which I stole for the love of the Gipsy boys!"

"Oh, where have you been, old mother, to-day?"
"Oh, I have been up at the farm, my boys;
    And I needn't say how
    I poisoned a sow,
And all for the love of the Gipsy boys!"

" Oh, where are you now, my fiddler lad ? "
" Oh, I am all here at hand, my boys ;
     And I'll scrape the strings,
     While the romali sings,
And all for the love of the Gipsy boys ! "

E. H. PALMER.

## O LIVINÉNGRÍ TEM.

———o———

Talla grya sār shan prástered, te o táttopen's avrī.
Sī the livinéngo chīrus for the póori Rómmani :
Well án, mi táchi pálya, if you've chīchī 'dré your fem.
Jāsa méngy kóttenescrus kéti Livinéngrī-tem.
        Mūkk amándi gíll ajā,
        Mūkk amandi gíll sār-sā—
    Sī the livinéngrī kedyin kennā !

Oh, i wéshor wéll safráni, te i rūzhior sove adré,
I pivlia shán sār brūni, te patrínya péll aláy :
Mā késsur for the rūzhior, mā késsur for the rūkk,
I livinéngrī rūzhior shan kūshtider to díck ;
        Yúl shán sā rínkeni—
        Mūkk's jāl sīg avrī :
    Sī the livinéngrī chīrus—āvali !

The kóshters hátch sār rūzno pensa kūroméngro mūsh,
An' the livinéngris kair len' būti sélno sim a wésh :
Oh, tūte'll kékker látcher a rínk'nodīro pem,
Te a tátto kūshto dívvus 'dré the Livinéngrī-tem.
        Oh, the dádas an' the dye,
        An' the chávo an' the chi—
    Adói sār'll lel sónnakai !

I livinéngror shan sā būti sūmeli ajā,
Tu'd pátser tu sos béshin 'drín a bōro kítchema :
Tu sūméssa kūshto lévinor kán tūte táders báv'—
Te o wáfro prástraméngro násti pūkk a chínger'n láv !
      Tūl the gry, tácho pal—
      Lel the tán avrī, mī chal :
    Amándi shom kāmmoben to jāl.

Kāna rātti véll' adói, ten amándi'll bésh aláy,
Mandy'll kair o yāg, an' pánder the kekāvi dóvapré ;
If Górgios pūkker " Sóssī ?" mándy'll rākker 'em—
    " Chīchī,
But a dróppus múttermengri for i chōri Rómmani ! "
      An' amándi'll kām to gíll,
      An we'll kūr an we'll kíll,
    An' sove 'dré the kālopen sār shíll.

Tálla sār the kédyin's kérdo, te mándy lels mī wye.
Mándy'll kin a rínk'no chúkko an' a shūba for mī chi ;
An mendūi'll kin trūshnīs to bíkin lángs o dróm :
Oh, the livinéngro chīrus sī būt kūshto for the Róm !
      Adrin o kālopen,
      Adrīn o shíllo wen,
    Mūkk's gílli o' the Livinéngrī-tem !
               JANET TUCKEY.

# KENT;

## OR, THE HOPPING-TIME.

——o——

When the summer-time is gone, and the races all are run,
Our luck's not over yet, for the hopping has begun :
So come, my Gipsy brothers, if everything is spent,
We'll all be off together to the pleasant land of Kent ;
     And we'll all sing in time,
     And we'll all sing in rhyme,
   A song of the merry hopping-time.

Oh, the flowers are fading fast, and the nuts are growing
   brown ;
The leaves are turning yellow, and the wind will blow
   them down ;
But no matter for the flower, and no matter for the tree,
The hops are all the flowers I would ever care to see ;
     They're the best of all that grow,
     So get up, lads, and go
   To the country where the hops hang low.

There the poles stand in line, like the men that serve the
Queen,
And the bines twist around them, and cover them with
green :
There's no prettier sight, let the rest be what they may,
Than a fine Kentish hop-field on a sunny autumn day.
　　　　Come, Gipsy boys so tall,
　　　　Come, Gipsy children small—
　　　There's money waiting yonder for us all !

Oh, the air smells so sweet where the ripe hop-blossoms
are,
You'd think you were sitting in a jolly alehouse bar ;
It's just like drinking beer in with every breath you
draw—
Oh, sure 'tis a wonder that it's not against the law !
　　　　Bring the horse and the tent—
　　　　We'll none of us repent
　　　Having gone to the pleasant land of Kent.

We'll pitch our little tent, and at night when work is
done,
We'll sit round the fire, and we'll hang the kettle on ;
And if Gorgios ask what's in it, we'll say, " What should
there be
In the poor Gipsies' kettle but a little drop of tea ? "

And we'll sing half the night,
And we'll dance and we'll fight,
Then we'll sleep till the sun rises bright.

When all the hops are picked, then we'll travel to the
town,
And I'll buy a coat, and my wife will buy a gown,
And we'll get a stock of baskets and sweeping-brushes
too :
Oh, the hopping keeps us going all the dreary winter
through.
So when nights are cold and long,
Let us sing loud and strong,
And remember the hopping in our song.

In answer to the common question, " How do Gipsies make
a living ?" I would say that during spring and summer they
attend races and fairs, or haunt picnics and merry-makings,
where their Aunt Sallys and cocoa-nuts are in demand, and
where fortune-telling and begging are tolerated, as giving
occasion for fun and raillery. When this happy time is over,
many of them go " hopping," and thus earn enough to lay in a
stock of baskets, clothes-lines, and similar wares. They then
wander all over England, each family taking its particular
" beat." As the men have less to do at this season, the ped-
dling baskets being entirely in the hands of the women, they
occupy themselves with " chinnin koshters," or cutting sticks,
*i.e.*, making *feeders* or clothes-pins and skewers. Sometimes
they make baskets, but this becomes every year more unusual
owing to the cheapness of French basket-ware. Those among

them who are more prosperous or intelligent deal in horses at all times, many becoming rich by the traffic. As a rule, Gipsies work hard and retire early. There is an impression that they subsist by stealing; but whatever the sins of their fathers may have been, the present generation does not generally deserve such a character. From what I have seen of Gipsies, I should say that they are, on the whole, as honest as the corresponding class of equally ignorant English people. They rarely betray a man who trusts them. I can recall, in relation to this, having once heard, from Mr Thomas Carlyle, an interesting anecdote of a Scottish Gipsy, who, having borrowed a sum of money, faithfully returned it. I have never heard of a "Rommany Rye" being robbed by a Gipsy.

# I SHŪNALI RAKLI.

—o—

Síg asā apré o Bōro Dívvus,
Kek'no gúdlo shūndom mán tasāla,
Áwer i pānéngri lóngodūro
Gíllyin 'dré o pūkkno, shíllo bāvol.

Sīg asā apré o Bōro Dívvus,
Múscro tamlopen te lūllo sāla,
Kána Chírki ghiás sār i chir'klor
Kána dūd anvías sāra hākus.

Vānka shūndom mé adré i wéshor,
Pénsa chóro mánūsh te martádas,
Te adénna chíngérben, te kórben,
Pénsa bōro hótcherin o' índi.

Sīgdum mé adói ta díck adúllo,
Te apré a bōro bar mé díckdom,
Pāsh o' léster wárdo hótchno sūrnī,
Véster Lock o Rómanny pūk'no béshdas.

Pútchdom : "Tūkey sī o dādas pūvdo,
Te hotchéssa tu kennā o vārdo,
Pénsa tácho Rómalo, Silvester :
Pénsa mōri pūreni Rómi fóki ?

" Ora tūkey sī ī kūshti dýa,
Sávo díckdas dré sā-būti wástor ?
Yoi te vél pen dūkkerin kékkūmi,
Sū viás la kéti hev, patsāva."

" Miro dáda sī kennā dré Lūndra ;
Mīnni dya si akái," yuv péndas,
" Mán hotcháva dul' pā jidi rākli,
Āwer mūllo sī sarjā améngy.

" Jāla lāki pūrus ; kéti ūtar,
Boro-panni-tem—shímál améngy,
Dúlla wāfri rākli sī améngy
Pūvdo, mūllo sī avrī te dívvus

" Méndi shánas kūrikus ta rúmmer ;
Bōro kūshto hālaben sos kédo ;
Líom mándy kūshtidīro cóvvar ;
(Móro Rómmano rye sārkān pessádas).

" Rya béshdas pré o bōro skámmin ;
Béshélla rashai apāsh o léste :
Vártem méndi sár apré Ótchámé ;
Āwer kek Ótchámé mén avélla.

" Sār sos chíngerdo, sārkān sos tūgno ;
Sār amándi ghiom adróm sār lájno,
Sīg sā méndi hādem mōro hābben,
Āwer kek Ótchámó men avélla.

" 'Pré tasāla shūndom lāki péndas,
Kédas les ta kair paiáss o méngi,
Te kamāva la sā boro-būti,
Man tevél nai kām ta mūkkov' lāti.

" Látchedem.   Péndas lāti sī atūkno,
Péndas yói te vél ta rúmma mándy,
Te o pāshno chīrus yói avélla
Kéti rūmmaben, te sīg te tácho.

" Āwer péndom : Sā sī chíkno bávol
Pré o drómya ; sā si lóndo pánni
Dré o dóeyav, mándy sovahal'lis,
Kékker men tevél te rúmmer túte.

" Sī sar kālo bal pré tiro shérro
Sos a sónnakeskro sūrni kúttor,
Man tevél kekūmi kāmer tūte ;
Būti shūnali shan tu amándy.

" Vóngustor te vél sār butī tūkey
Sā o spíngor lela hótchewitchi,
Pórdo sāro sónnakéskro covvár,
Mándy jāva 'vrī kún tūte vías.

" Te pā dúllo gúdlo tú man kédas.
Te pā dúlla lávya tu penéssa,
Shánas tu sarjā amóngy mūllo,
Kána mūshor pen'lan tūte jído.

" Te pā mándy tūte sás sā wáfro,
Kédas méngy dúllo dúshno gúdlo,
Mándy hotcherōv 'o kūshto várdo
Sávo mándy péndom dél a tūkey."

Róvades.   Amén o wáver géeror
Sávo atchdé 'dói to shūn a léste,
Díkdom mé a Górgio hatchélla,
Te o Górgio rovés asárla.

Pútchdom : " Sī o rākkerben, mi-rýa
Sávo anneréla dúllo pánni
Tīri yākkor ; sā o tūv, te késsur,
Káiren tūte bōro wáfro tūknus ? "

Āwer péndas : " Mándy kek kessāva
Pā lo tūv, te chīchi pā o rākker,
Āwer bíkdom dovo várdo léski
Pátserdo.—te yúv te vél kek péssur ! "

Tácho sos o láv, te sī—te kékker,
Sā o panni dóeyav sī pordo,
Léla Górgio a yéckno hārra
Fon o Rómalo, sār zi-poggádo.

CHARLES G. LELAND.

# THE WILFUL GIRL.

So early on Christmas morning,
   No other sound was there,
But bells far off a-ringing
   Through the silent frosty air.

So early on Christmas morning,
   Between the dark and dawn,
When the stars were going like pigeons,
   As the day like a hawk came on ;

I heard a noise in the forest,
   The voice of a wailing man ;
And then a rustling, crackling,
   As though a fire began.

I hurried to the burning,
   And there upon a rock,
Beside his blazing waggon,
   Sat the Gipsy Vester Lock.

E

" Oh, have you buried your father?
    And, like a Rommany true,
Are you burning up his waggon,
    As the real old Rommanis do ?

" Or is it your good old mother,
    Who looked in so many a hand ?
She will read no more the future
    Since she's gone to the future land."

" My father is still in London,
    And my mother is here," said he.
" This is burnt for a girl who is living,
    But dead for ever to me.

" And whether she walk the South or West,
    Or live by East or North,
That wicked girl is in her grave
    To me from this day forth.

" Last week we were to marry,
    With a dinner and a ball ;
And our Rommany *rye*—you know him—
    Got it ready, and paid for all !

" The *rye* was on the sofa,
    The priest was in his chair ;
We waited for Otchamé,
    But Otchamé was not there.

"So it all broke up in sorrow,
　And we all went off in shame,
(Though we stayed till dinner was over),
　Otchamé never came.

"And I heard that she said she did it
　Because I loved her so,
That for twice the trick and trouble
　I never would let her go.

"We met, and she said she was sorry,—
　That I still should be her *rom*,
And the next time to the wedding
　She would really be sure to come !

"But I said: While there's dust on the highway,
　And water is in the sea,
There will never be a wedding
　In the world between you and me.

"If every hair of your ringlets
　Was a spangle of shining gold,
I never would ask to marry
　A maiden so bad and bold.

"If you had as many fingers
　As a hedgehog has pins to show,
And all with rings close crowded,
　Whenever you came I'd go.

" And because you have been so cruel,
  And served me such a turn,
I've a waggon I meant to give you,
  And now that waggon I'll burn."

He wept, and among the people
  Who had stayed to hear him through,
I saw a Gentile standing,
  And the Gentile was weeping too.

And I asked him, "Is it the story
  Which causes the tears to rise?
Or the smoke of the burning waggon
  That so affects your eyes?"

He answered, "I'm not affected
  By the smoke nor by what he said;
But I sold him that waggon on credit,
  And I know I shall never be paid."

No more he wasn't, and never,
  While water is in the sea,
Will he ever get a copper
  From the heart-broken Rommany.

CHARLES G. LELAND.

English Gipsies not only frequently burn or destroy all that belonged to their dead relations, but sometimes, when urged by strong emotions, make sacrifices like the one de-

scribed in the foregoing ballad. It is all literally true, even
to the remark as to the hairs of the head being spangles.
The only liberty taken with the truth has been in making
the unfortunate man from whom the waggon was purchased
a weeping eye-witness. It is, however, a fact that this highly
interesting sacrifice was entirely "upon tick." I have omitted
to state that the mortified lover also broke his watch to fragments; but, with some of the inconsistency characteristic of
Gipsies, Indians, and other grown-up children, he carefully
collected and sold the fragments, as well as the iron portions
of the waggon.

# O RÓMMANÉSTO KÉLLOBEN.

——o——

Pāsh-a-shél o' kālo Rómmanis in kūshto dickin heesis,
Pāsh-a-shél o' kālo Rommanis with wongur in their
    keesis,
    A-wéllin sāro kétteni and pénnin sārishán ;
Pāsh o' lendy Beshaláys and pāsh o lendy Petuléngros,
Tachodīro kālo Rommanis and fino kélloméngros,
    A wéllin 'dré the gav to lel a kéllamésto tan.

Būtidósta Górgio mūshor kāmed ta díckavit adóvo,
Yól délled the kālo-rāti fóki sār o léndy's lóvo,
    Te the chálor mūkked the Górgio mūshor. hav adré
    the kér.
The ráklis sos a kéllin, a sávvyin and a gíllin,
The pūri dye a shéllin, and the bóshermengro kíllin ;
    Oh ! to dick a wāver rāti sim adóvo m'an'y'd mer.

The hábben lis sos kūshto te o pīopen sos tátto,
Te páller bitti chīrus sār the cháls and chais sos mātto,
    An' the paiāss sos the kūshtidīrest tūte 'd ever dick,
Sīggadīro kélled the tánis, sīgger killed the bosherméngro,
Till the Beshaláy-sheréngro wélled atūt the Petuléngro,
    An' yúv an' lósters chai sos wūssed aláy opré the chick.

Pāl 'adóvo sos a chíngari apósh adóvo dūi,

Te the Petuléngro kūred the Beshaláy oprè the mūi ;

Te the dūi ráklis tádered yek-a-wāver by the bál.

Te the wāver mūshor prástered up to hátch oprè their
pálor,

Te milled opré a-kūrin sor the chior and the chálor,

Te they mūkked the bósh and kélloben to kūr an'
sóvahāl.


Oh, 'dói sos shérros póggado, te rink'ni kāli yākkor,

Te lūllo mol a wéllin out o' kāli chávvos nākkor,

Te the cūrror and the chauros wūssin sār adrè the báv.

Te the Górgio ryes an' rānīs prästeréllan for their
mériben,

Te the rátfully chokéngros wélled to lell us sār to stari-
ben,

Tūte sasti pen the beng sos jāllin loosus in the gáv.


Te kána lén sos kínlo, up the Petuléngro prästers,

Te chivs his dūi wasts adrè the wāver geero's wāsters,

Te chūmers lésters chámyor—sā they kaired lis sor
oprè :

Te they bitchered for some lívènor an' delled it to the
bālor,

Te piid te kélled againus till the wéllin o' the sālor,

Then they pelt oprè the pūvus, an' they sóvelan aláy.

Now dóvo's sāvo mandy pens a kūshto sort o' cóvva,
For we'd lévina te páiass an' we kaired adósta lóvo ;
   An' as for kālor yākkor, dóvo's rínkeno ajā !
For the chíngeri sos bítti, but the páiass it was bōro,
An' I pens adóvo sims a bitti lon oprè the mōro ;
   An' if tūte'll dell a kélloben I'm kāmmoben to jā !

E. H. Palmer.

# THE GIPSY BALL.

FIFTY dusky Rommanis dressed so fine and grand, sir ;
Fifty dusky Rommanis with money at command, sir,
  A-meetin' and a-greetin' in the village one and all.
Half o' them was Smith and t'other half of 'em was
    Stanley,
Gipsies out and out, and dancers elegant and manly,
  Comin' in the town to hire a place to give a ball.

Lots o' Gorgio people longed to see a sight so funny,
So they gave the dark-faced Gipsies pretty nearly all
    their money ;
  And the Rommanis they let the Gorgio gentry
    come inside.
The girls they was a dancin' and a laughin' and a hum-
    min',
The grandmothers a chaffin', and the music band a
    strummin'—
  Oh ! to see another such a night as that I would ha'
    died.

The victuals they was first-rate, and the drink was
first-rate, very;
And 'twasn't very long afore the boys and girls got
merry;
And the sport it was the best you ever see, sir, I'll
be bound.
Faster danced the ladies, and the fiddler fiddled
faster,
Till the captain of the Stanleys and the Smiths' head
man and master
Bumped one agin the other and was thrown upon
the ground.


And then there was a shindy very quickly in the place,
sir,
The Smith he gave the Stanley such a oner in the face,
sir,
And their partners took to tearing one another by
the hair.
Then the men of both the parties came up each to help
his brother,
And the lads and lasses fought and all got mixed with
one another,
And they left the dance and music and began to
fight and swear.

Oh ! the broken heads and black eyes which they got,
    sir, it was stunnin',
And the claret from their noses pretty freely was a
    runnin',
        An' the pewters and the platters was a flyin' by
        your face.
The Gorgios ran away when the row had first
    arisen,
An' the bobbies they came runnin' up to take us all to
    prison—
        You'd ha' said the very deuce was broken loose
        about the place.


When they all was tired o' fightin', the Smith he made
    a stand, sir,
And he come up to the other chap and shook him by
    the hand, sir,
        And kissed him on the cheek and made it up for
        evermore.
Then they sent and fetched some more beer, and they
    give it to the Runners,
And they drank and danced again, until the mornin'
    broke, like oners,
        And then they all fell down and went to sleep upon
        the floor.

Now that's what I should call a werry pleasant sort o'
party,
For we'd beer, and made some money, and enjoyed ourselves quite hearty,
And as for black eyes, why black eyes are pretty as
you'know !
For the row was only little, and the fun was werry great,
sir,
Just like a pinch o' salt upon your bread, I calculate,
sir,
And if you'll give another ball, why I am game
to go.

E. H. PALMER.

This description of a ball was given to Professor Palmer by an
eye-witness. The dance in question was held at Aberystwith.
Of late years Gipsies often give these balls, charging a price
for admission. They are, in reality, Gipsy exhibitions.

# A TÁCHO CÓVVABEN;

OR, O ROMMANI BENG.

———o———

OH, tūte jins mīro kāko, rye,
  Oh, tūte jins lester náv ;
Yeck dívvus yúv pīrdas sār léster gry
  Fon yeck 'eti wāver gáv.

Yúv jássed adré a kitchema
  To pī a tás lévinor ;
But o pūro gry lellas chīchī to hā
  But o wáfro chár túller o bor.

Būt' lévinor kairs a mūsh súrrelo,
  An' mī kāko gillied sār 'sār,
Āwer lester gry sos bóckelo,
  Te sā yúv pīrīed shūkár.

Penned o Rom, "Kán' a mūsh lels adústa mās,
  Yúv givella kūshto ajā,
Te lélldas tūte a bítti káss,
  Tu'd pīrri sirān, mī bā !

"Dóv é lo, mīro gry, dóv é lo?
'Drin pūv, 'pré o wāver rikk
O bor, sī a bōro kássengro,
Te kekker adói to dick."

Akóvalo Rom jās míshto ajā
To hócker adrín o pūv:
Yúv násti jínav a wāver mūsh
Chídas lester yākkor 'pré yúv.

A tāno, bóngo, kálo chál
Sos béshin táller o kosh:
Mīro kāko péndas yúv kékker jin's
S' a wáfro-díckeno mūsh.

Mī kāko sos gíllyin—"Kūshto bak!"
Āwer sīg yúv tūldas chib,
For o pūro chávo hóckered apré,
An' shelled in Rómmani jib:

"Beng tásser tūte, tu wáfro chál!
So's tūte kairin kennā?
Man bítcheráv' tūt' to stáripen,
For chórin mī káss ajā."

Mī pooro kāko sos trásheno:
Yuv pūkkeras—"So-sī lis?
Dórdi!—o béngis own kókero,
'S a-rákkerin Rommanis!"

Tácho, mī rýa, yúv násti hátch
  A-pūkkerin Sārishán,
Awer hūtered apré an' kístered avri,
  Till yuv látched o Rómmani tán.

Te adói yúv péndas : "Deari pals
  Kána tūte jāsa to chore,
Dick firstus if a Rómmani beng
  Kek béshela táller o bor!"

JANET TUCKEY.

# A REAL INCIDENT.

I'M thinking you know my uncle, sir,
  And you know his name, I'll be bound.
The other day his horse and he
  Were travelling the country round.

My uncle went to a public-house,
  And there he got beer enough;
But the poor old horse had nothing to eat
  But nettles and such like stuff.

Oh, beer is the thing to cheer one's heart,
  So my uncle whistled a song;
But the poor old horse had little to eat,
  So he went but slowly along.

Said the man, " When a man has enough o' meat,
  He whistles aloud for joy,
And if you'd a mouthful of hay to eat,
  You'd go faster than this, my boy !

" What is that, my horse ; oh, what is that ?
  On the other side of the way,
With never a soul a watching it,
  There's a beautiful stack of hay ! "

So this my Gipsy loses no time
  A jumping over the stile ;
He didn't guess there was somebody
  A watching him all the while.

A little, crooked, yellow-faced man
  Was sitting beneath a tree ;
My uncle told me he'd ne'er beheld
  Such an ugly fellow as he.

My uncle was singing " Good luck, good luck ! "
  But he soon let singing alone,
For the man jumped up and hollered at him,
  In Rommany like his own—

" Deil take you, mischievous good-for-nought !
  That game you are at won't pay ;
I'll get you a month, and no mistake,
  For stealing of that there hay ! "

My uncle was frightened out of his wits,
  He cried, " What is it I see ?
That ugly chap is the deil's own self
  A swearing in Rommany ! "

You may take your oath that he didn't stop
A saying of, How do you do ?
But he jumped on his horse and galloped like mad,
Till he got to some tents he knew.

And he said, " My lads, when you're going to steal,
Take this bit of advice from me—
Just find out first if some Gipsy deil
Ain't watching you under a tree ! "

JANET TUCKEY.

The incident related in this ballad is given, with the exception of rhyme and metre, in almost the same words in which it was told. It should be mentioned, however, that the old Gipsy who contemplated stealing the hay, invariably denies that anything of the kind ever took place. But as his Rommany friends are fond of " chafling" him about the " Gipsy devil," and as he himself will sometimes, with a grave face, insist that he never heard the story, it is probably true. In Rommany *one* negative is generally equivalent to an affirmative.

# O RÓMMANI CHÍRICLO.

———o———

Rómmani chíriclo 'prė o rūkk,
Shūnalo Rómmani chíriclo pūkk,
Gívelliu kūshto, gívellin sār,
Wāvero chíriclo tállera bor.

" Pal, so's tūte díckdo kennā,
Te tū ghivéssa sā kūshto ajā ? "
" Tállero rūkk kái mándy shom
Rínkeni rāni rovéll' adróm.

" Lāki sī kékeni pirrýno ;
Chūredīr sī ténna chíriclo ;
Sī bōro tūg' adré lāki zī,
Kércla pánni násher avrī.

" Āwer, mīpal, yeck mī fon akái.
Túlla wāver rūkk beshélla rye :
Yúv te dél pāsh o' yúvs wóngur adróm
Te vel 'dúlla rínkeni rānis rom."

" Oh, mīro pal, sos táchenus
Kairav i dūi kéttenus !
Yeck pirrýni te yeck pirrýno ! "
" Awer sā ésti tūte kairavit so ? "

" Beshélla rāni 'dré bōro tūv ;
Lākis pāno dikklo's apré o pūv ;
Chorāva lis, te mūkker' avrī,
Ta lel lis avélla pāli mī.

" Te vel pállerélla mán ap' an' aláy,
Awer kekera dāva lis apré
Tálla hăpperāva lā fon akái,
Te síkkerava la rūzlo rye.

" Te kūshto asā o mīli rye,
T'vel rākker sā tácho i gúdli chi :
Awer kāmescri te kāmescró
Nástis jín sos kérdo o chíriclo."

CHARLES G. LELAND.

## THE GIPSY-BIRD.

THE Gipsy-bird sits on the oak-branch high,
And talks to his mate on the hedge hard by ;
He's singing loudly, he's singing well —
Hear what the Gipsy-bird has to tell.

His mate says, " What is the matter, dear,
That you sing so loud, that you sing so clear ? "
" I sing, because under this very bough,
A beautiful lady is resting now.

" She's all by herself, no mate has she,
No bird in the wood so poor can be ;
Her heart is heavy with grief, I know,
For I am watching her tears that flow.

" But listen, a mile from here I see
A youth sits under another tree ;
He'd give the half of his gold and land
To win such a beautiful lady's hand."

" Little wife, it were a good deed, in truth,
To bring them together, the maid and youth ;
And of the two to make but one ! "
" Pleasant to do, if it could be done."

" Look down, little wife ; on the grass below
Is the lady's handkerchief white as snow :
I'll hasten to steal it, and on my track
She'll surely follow, to get it back.

" And I'll lead her on over brier and fern ;
I'll never stop and I'll never turn,
Nor let her linger through all the chase,
Till she and the youth shall be face to face.

" Then never again will she weep alone,
For he'll woo her softly to be his own,
And she'll answer him back with a softer word,
But they never will know it was done by the bird."

JANET TUCKEY.

The Gipsy-bird, or Water-wagtail, can hardly be correctly spoken of as *singing*. But both in Germany and England, Gipsies regard it as belonging peculiarly to them, and attach strange superstitions to it. Thus they believe that it portends the presence of Gipsies, and whenever a traveller sees it he will meet with the Rommany not long after. The *Kipsi Kasht*, or willow, is the Gipsy-tree.

# BÁLLOVAS AN YÓRAS.

—o—

BÁLLOVAS *an yóras,*
*Bállovas an yóras,*
*An the rye an the rāni*
　　*A pīrryin āp the drom.*
If tūtes mándys pírrynī,
If tūte's miri pīrrynī,
Te well tu mándy's pīrrynī,
　　Then mándy'll be your Rom.


Mándy latched a hotchewítchi,
A bōro hotchewítchi;
A tūllo hotchewítchi,
　　A jāllin 'dré the wésh.
'Dói welldé rye te rāni,
O kūshto rye te rāni,
An' adói, 'tūll the rūkkor;
　　Mándy dicked the dūi besh.

Yúl kékn'ai jíndé mándy,
Yúl kékn'ai pénd'te mándy,
Yúl násti shūndé mándy
        Díkdom sār o léndy kaired :
If they jínned I dicked the chūmors
The kūshti bitti chūmors
If they'd jínned I shūned the chūmors
        Oh !—the rāni would a-méred.


Oh, hátchin ain't a-hóckerin,
An' gíllyin ain't rākkerin,
An' gíllyin ain't pūkkerin,
        Penāva mán asā.
So leláv akóvo kūnjernes,
Rikkāva lis sār kūnjernes,
Rikkāv' akóvo kūnjernes—
        Sā tu shūnéssa k'nā.

                        CHARLES G. LELAND.

# EGGS AND BACON.

———o———

OH ! the eggs and bacon ;
And oh ! the eggs and bacon ;
And the gentleman and lady
    A walking up the way !
And if you will be my sweetheart,
And if you will be my sweetheart,
And if you will be my darling,
    I will be your own, to-day.


Oh ! I found a jolly hedgehog ;
Oh ! I found a good fat hedgehog ;
Oh ! I found a good big hedgehog,
    In the wood beyond the town :
And there came the lord and lady,
The handsome lord and lady,
And underneath the branches
    I saw the two sit down.

They didn't know the Gipsy,
They didn't think the Gipsy,
They didn't hear the Gipsy
    Was looking—or could hide.
If they knew I saw the kisses,
The pretty little kisses,
If they knew I heard the kisses,
    Oh, the lady would ha' died !


Oh ! sitting still's not springing,
And talking isn't singing,
So I tell you nothing, singing,
    That's the way I make it square.
So I keep this thing a secret,
I keep it all a secret,
A very sacred secret,
    As all of you can hear.

                      CHARLES G. LELAND.

A part of this trifling song is of Gipsy origin, and well known to most "travellers." The remainder was composed one day in a tent on the banks of the Thames, with the help of several Gipsies, who greatly admired the rhymes, especially those contributed by themselves. Nothing can be said for it, except that it gives a tolerably correct idea of the style of much Rommany singing.

# MÁNSHA TU!

———o———

Mɪ ghiom a-pīrraben 'pré o drom,
Shūndom a kālo-rattéscro Rom,
Yúv gillides kūshto, yúv gíll'des ajā—
" Sóssī mandy to kair kennā?
    Mánsha tu, pal, mánsha tu !
    O bāk avélla tasāla.

" Mīro bítto wárdo sī hótchado ;
Li'sos sā būti rínkeno—
'Pré mínno láv, mī Rómmani láv,
Kék sā kūshto adrín o gáv.
    Mánsha tu, pal, mánsha tu !
    O bāk avélla tasāla.

" 'Dré o rātti li'sos hótchado ;
Adóvo dūd sos rínkeno !
I bítti chíngaror mūkkered avrī,
Kéti Midúvelus-tem apré.
    Mánsha tu, pal, mánsha tu
    O bāk avélla tasāla."

" So-sī tu gívellin, mīro pal ?
Sī wáfro cóvva, mí kālo chál !
Sos man te vel tūte, rovāv' o' dúsh——
" Áver tūte shán kék Rómmani mūsh !
        Mánsha tu, pal, mánsha tu !
        O bāk avélla tasāla.

" Sóski Rómmani chál to rúv ?
Yéckorus, 'drín o givéscro pūv,
Mi chórdom mýla, i mýla méred—
Pūkkeras tūte so mándy kaired ?
        Mánsha tu, pal, mánsha tu !
        O bāk avélla tasāla.

" A rāni díckdas mándy bésh
Pāsh i mūllo mýla adrín o wésh :
' Yúvs pal sī mūllo', péndas adróm—
' O chóro, páuvero, kālo Rom ! '
        Mánsha tu, pal, mánsha tu !
        O bāk avélla tasāla.

" Yói sos a gúdli, bárveli chi —
Dás méngy lóvva tu kin a gry ;
Aver mi chórdom a gry ajā,
Te kíndom wárdo kún's náshered kennā.
        Mánsha tu, pal, mánsha tu !
        O bāk avélla tasāla.

" Táller o bor beshāv' shūkár,
Gívellin kūshto sārasār,
Te mīro gry, oh, kai sī yúv ?
Chórin lescro hābben adrín o pūv !
    Mánsha tu, pal, mánsha tu !
    O bāk avélla tasāla.

" Givāva mándy adróm, mi rye,
A gúdlo cóvva avéll' akái,
For kūshto bāk sī o tácho pal
Kéti míshto, rūzno Rómmani chál.
    Mánsha tu, pal, mánsha tu !
    O bāk avélla tasāla."

JANET TUCKEY.

# CHEER UP!

———o———

ALONG the road I was wandering,
When I heard a brown-faced Gipsy sing—
" Oh dear, my drag is burnt and gone !
Who can tell me what's to be done ?
    Cheer up, brother, never sorrow !
    Luck will come again to-morrow.

" Search everywhere, search up and down,
You'll find none better in all the town ;
Upon my word, my Rommany word,
That waggon of mine was fit for a lord.
    Cheer up, brother, never sorrow !
    Luck will come again to-morrow.

" 'Twas burnt up only yesternight ;
You've never seen a fire so bright ;
The sparks flew out, flew up so high,
They didn't stop till they touched the sky.
    Cheer up, brother, never sorrow !
    Luck will come again to-morrow."

Said I, " Your story is full of woe,
Then why do you sing, I'd like to know ?
If I were you, I couldn't be glad—— "
" But, sir, you're not a Rommany lad.
  Cheer up, brother, never sorrow !
  Luck will come again to-morrow.

" Why should a merry Gipsy weep ?
Once, when the farmer was fast asleep,
I stole an ass, but soon she died :
I sat me down by that donkey's side.
  Cheer up, brother, never sorrow !
  Luck will come again to-morrow.

" A Gorgio lady came through the wood,
The Gorgio lady was rich and good.
She looked at my donkey, she looked at me ;
' Oh, the Gipsy's friend is dead,' said she.
  Cheer up, brother, never sorrow !
  Luck will come again to-morrow.

" She gave me a purse, a beautiful purse,
Lots of money to buy a horse ;
But I stole a horse, as I well knew how,
And bought the waggon that's burnt up now.
  Cheer up, brother, never sorrow !
  Luck will come again to-morrow.

" Under the hedge at my ease I'll stay,
Singing so jolly the livelong day.
My horse is a Rommany, just like me,
He's stealing the farmer's oats, you see.
    Cheer up, brother, never sorrow !
    Luck will come again to-morrow.

" If you care for nothing, you needn't doubt
But luck will come by and will find you out ;
For jolly good luck, as you well may see,
Is a friend to the regular Rommany.
    Cheer up, brother, never sorrow,
    Luck will come again to-morrow."

                       JANET TUCKEY.

The incident here described is substantially the same as one narrated by an old Gipsy in Surrey as having occurred to himself.  In justice to the old man, it should be admitted that the theft of the donkey and horse is a poetic fiction.

—o—

YECK dívvus pīrdum mé trin-desh mceya sār mīro pūro Pīrengro, parl chūmbor te hévya, dickin Róm-mani kairéngror adré bitti gávya, ora rākkerin apré pūri chīruses. Kennādoi yuv sīkkerdas méngy a tan adré o chār, kai a Gorgio te well dick chi-chi, āwer odoi yúv sikkerdas méngy sikko, kai yuv's pal o kāko beshedé alay, sásti beshya kennā. Sā mendūi ghiom pāsh 'Ginny Pánni, te parl o Stans Chūmber, te Staines, kai a wāver kūshto pál o mándy kairdas a bōro kūraben apré ye prásterin o 'ye grya, te so viom án kérri, kéti mīro Boro Kitchema, návvo Giv-Puvior, 'pré o Borgav, te yuv rikkerdas mīro chúkko. Āwer sā sīg mendūi pīrressa, ghiom amánde agāl būti kūsi kítche-mor, talla jāllin adré, for mīro chúkko boried pāsher a bar, sā denne mīro rikkerin-mūsh kāmdas kennādoi a cutter o levinor. Kennāsig apré ye nāk o' the dívvus, mīro pūro pál ānkairdas ta mizzer te mújer lis adré léster shérro, te mándy lelledum a drúm o' déllin léscro a pāsh koránna. Te sā yuv sos a kellin

G

an ludderin lestis kokero apré the drom, givelldas yuv adré a būti paiáscro shūnaben akovo givelli—

" Mándy's chávvis shan bokelo—ókelo—kókelo.
Shan mūllerin o' shíllaben—híllaben—íllaben.
Yul lena lek hābben—obbin—abobbin
Shan pauveri, te chúvveni—púvveni—húvveny
Man'ys bitto tan sī chíngerdo—híngerdo—bíngerdo
Sī sār in cútter-éngerees—mingerees—fingerees.
O shillo bávol pūderla 'dré ye hévyor—shévyor,
Sārráti mándy shūnova ye wāfo bávo bávela.
Sárrāti mendūi rúvv, mérin for mōro pré the púv.
Man'ys chávvis got kek dye ; high de dy, dy dy !
Diddle dum dum.
Mandy'd die if 'twasn't for mīro kūshto rye !
Diddle dum dum, dum dum,
Diddle, dim dam dum.
Mándy's a chúredo—húrredo—kúrredo.
High diddle diddle ! "

Te sā mendūi viom keti kunsus o' the drum, diom mé lésco lesters pāsh koránna. Te o pūro mūsh kairedas kin, te ghias kérri, sā kūmi te kūshto sā bokro.

CHARLES G. LELAND.

# THE SONG OF STARVATION.

---o---

ONE day I went thirty miles a-foot with my old Walker, across hills and dales, calling on Gipsy house-dwellers in the little villages, or talking over old times as we went. Now and then he would point out a place in the grass where a Górgio (white man) could see nothing, but there he would show me exactly where his brother or uncle had camped, perhaps years ago. So we two passed by Virginia Water, and across Saint Ann's Hill, and through Staines, where another good friend of mine had a great fight at the last races, and then went homeward to my hotel, called Oatlands, near Walton. And he carried my coat. But as we walked, we passed very few public-houses without going in, for my coat weighed almost a pound, and my carrier, of course, needed now and then a drop of ale. By and by, towards the end of the day, my old friend began to turn it over in his head, and reflect that I had a way of giving him a half-crown; and, to remind me of it, while

he was dancing and shaking himself on the road, he
sang, in a very jolly voice, this song—

" My children are hungry—bungry—wungry,
    They're dying of the bitter cold—diddle diddle dum.
    They haven't any victuals—skittles—tittles,
    They're perishing in poverty—tum teedle tum!
    My little tent's in tatters—hatters—scatters,
    All in rags a-flyin'—highin'—skyin'.
    The cold wind a-blowin'—lowin'—owin',
    All night I hear it whistle—sissel—diddle.
    All night we're a-cryin'—for a bit o' bread a-dyin'.
    My babes ha' got no mother—nor father—nother.
    Certainly I should die, but for my master standing by.
    I am poor—boor—oor!
    Diddle dum dum, dum dum,
    Diddle, dim—dam—dum,
    High diddle diddle."

And when we came to the end (corner) of the road, I
gave him his half-crown.  So the old fellow got off the
road, and went home as quiet and good as a lamb.

                                        CHARLES G. LELAND.

# TÁCHIPEN AND WÁFODIPEN.

———o———

MAN dickdum a Rommany 'drè the tán,
Te péndum lestc " Sārishan ? "
Yúv sávvdas amándy and shélled avrī,
" Avali, pāla, kūshto sī !
Shom mātto sā būti a rye should be."

I chávvi kairdas the yāg oprè,
O tūvus welldas the tan adrè,
" Oh, béngis the rátfūlly tūvis zī !
A wéllin adré mi yākk ! " pens he,
Sa mātto sā būti a rye could be.

Out of the tan avrī he wells
The bósh an' the kósht in his vást he lells :
Te 'prè the chār beshélla he,
Gillin adróm in Rommany,
Sā mātto sā būti a rye should be.

The górgiky mūshor wélled án to dick ;
Beshéllan léndy opré the chick,

Ta shūn lis gíll adré Rommany;
"Dordi!" penéllan, "Mister Lee,
Sī mātto sā būti a rye can be."

Léskri chávvi sos hátchin adói;
Shūnélla givelli, rovélla yói,
" Mā mūkklis giller !" yói shélls avrī,
" A-síkkerin Górgios Rómmany—
Sā mātto sā būti a mūsh can be."

Péndom a láv 'drin léster's kán,
Te lélled the Rommany 'dré the tan :
" Dórdi's a kālor ! bitcher avrī
For a cúrro livenor mūkkelas pī,
Till améndi's mātto as ryes should be."

The wāver kúrikus a rashái
Sār a kālo rūdaben vias akái,
Te péndas : "Lessa kek sīg ta pī."
Pens man'y, " Adóvo 'sī hóckeny
Tūte kok'ro's mātto as yeck can be ! "

I kāms to díckavit Rómmany chals
Gíllin te kíllin sār léndy's páls :
But I péns as acóvvo sī wáffodí
To rākker the jib kai Górgios sī,
If a mūsh *is* as mātto as yuv can be.

E. H. PALMER.

# GIPSY MORALS.

A GIPSY lad in his tent did lie :
" How do ye do, my boy ? " said I.
He laughs outright, and says, says he,
" Things is a-goin' all right with me,
I'm drunk as a gentleman need to be ! "

The girl she gave the fire a poke ;
Into the tent came clouds of smoke ;
" Bother it ! I can hardly see,
The smoke has got into my eyes," says he,
As drunk as a gentleman need to be.

Out of the tent he bundles quick,
And takes the fiddle and fiddlestick ;
Down on the grass outside sits he,
Singing away in Rommany—
As drunk as a gentleman need to be.

The Gorgios, when they heard the sound,
Came running up, and crowded round
To hear him sing in Rommany,

Crying, " Oh, look at Mister Lee,
Drunk as a gentleman need to be ! "

The Gipsy's daughter was standing by,
And, hearing him sing, began to cry ;
" Oh ! stop his singin'," she says, says she,
" A-teachin' of Gorgios Rommany—
As drunk as ever a man can be."

I went and whispered in his ear,
Took him inside to have some beer ;
Says I, " I've got a shillin', see !
Send for a gallon, and you and me
Will drink till we're drunk as gents should be."

I saw a clergyman t'other week,
A black-coat fellow with lots of cheek ;
" You oughtn't to drink no beer," said he ;
Says I, " You're a-tellin' a lie to me,
You're as drunk yourself as a man can be."

I loves to see a Gipsy lad
A-singin' and playin' away like mad ;
But this is what seems a sin to me,
To talk afore Gorgios in Rommany,
If a man *is* as drunk as a man can be.

E. H. PALMER.

---

The above scene was witnessed by Prof. Palmer, and is exactly described in the ballad.

# KAIRIN KĀMMOBEN.

*(Adré o pūro chīrus.)*

—o—

I PŪRI dye sī jíllo
   Ke 'dóvo gáv kennā ;
O pūro dád' beshélla
   Adrín o kítchemā ;
Kek mūsh 'dré sār o tánya,
   Kek chí to pūkk a lav :
Mi shom akái, akónyo—
   Áv, mīro kāmlo, áv !
     Dórdi, sossī mandy kairin
     Pāsh o lūllo yāg ?
     Būti, būti, sār pa tūte,
     Túkey kūshto bāk !

Mi dūkkerdum i rāni
   'Dré 'dóvo bōro kér :
Kek kāli chovihāni
   Vel kair lis kūshtider.

Man pūkkdom' rink'ni cóvva,
A bárv'lo rye, te sā :
Yói das a-méngy lóvva,
Mi pórdowast ajā.
Oh, mi sósti rākker, dūkker
Górgios adróm,
Būti, būti, sār pa tūte
Mīro kāmlo rom !

Oh, Rómmanis shan jónger !
Mi shom kek dínneli chi :
Mi gáverdum o wóngur,
Te kek'no jíndas kai.
Mi kíndum kūshto vōro,
Irātti, kūnjernī :
O móriclo sī kérro—
Av, deari, tácho sī !
Pāno vōro, pāno lóvva,
'Drín a móriclo,
Būti, būti, sār pa tūte,
Kāmlo pīrrýno !

Hátch pāl' o bor, mo chávo—
Hátch pūkeno pāli lis :
Kennā mán tūt' avāva,
Sār sīg o Rómmanis :

Avāva, pál, ta wūsser
  O mor'clo 'tūt o bor ;
Oh, tūte ásti péssur
  Adústa lévinor.
    Lel a chūmer, del a chūmer ?
     Āvo, āvali !
    Būti, būti, sār pa tūte,
     Mīro kāmlo zī !

JANET TUCKEY.

# GIPSY LOVE-MAKING.

## (*In the old time.*)

—*o*—

My mother's gone a-wandering
 Away to yonder town ;
My father in the alehouse
 Is safely settled down ;
There's not a girl to gossip ;
 There's not a lad at home :
I'm all alone and waiting—
 So come, my darling, come !
  Tell me what I'm doing
  By the fire-light here,
 All for you, love, all for true love,
  All for luck, my dear.

I told a lady's fortune
 In that big house hard by :
No Gipsy could have done it
 More cleverly than I ;

I promised that she'd marry
 A lord with heaps of gold ;
She filled my hand with silver,
 As much as I could hold.
  I can chatter, flatter
   Gorgios far and near,
   All for you, love, all for true love.
   All for luck, my dear !

Oh, Rommanis are cunning !
 I know what I'm about ;
I hid away the money,
 Where no one found it out.
I bought some flour last evening—
 I bought it secretly ;
Come, now the cake is ready.
 And nobody to see.
  Meal so white, money bright,
   Baked together here,
   All for you, love, all for true love,
   All for luck, my dear !

Wait near the hedge awhile, lad,
 Stay yet a moment, stay—
I'm coming now to meet you,
 In our old Gipsy way.

I'll throw the cake right over,
Although the hedge is high :
Go, drink to me, my lover,
Go—drink the tavern dry !
What is this ? First a kiss ?—
Plenty, never fear ;
All for you, love, all for true love.
All for luck, my dear !

JANET TUCKEY.

It would appear, from an account given by an old Gipsy woman, that formerly, in Rommany wooing, the more valuable gifts were made by the girls, possibly as a proof of their ability to contribute to the expenses of married life. She laid especial stress on the fact that the damsels would hide as much money as they could out of their earnings, and bake it in a cake, which was usually thrown over the hedge to the expectant lover. Among such people, courtship reduces itself to very simple principles.

# JŪKALO ROMMANIS.

—o—

YECK Rómmani chál te a Górgio,
  Ye pūri dyéskri dye,
Pánj chávor, te a geero—
  A chūreno dídikai :
Awer o Rom sos rūzno,
  An' bōro apré the chib,
Te shordas sā léster kókero,
  'S deep'dīrus 'dré Rómmani jib.


I dye sos kāli Rómni,
  Te a bitto húnnalo ;
O chūredo rīkkerdas stádī,
  Sos kek'nai būt' súrrelo ;
Āv' o Rómmani mūsh sos búno,
  Te díckdas sārjā avrī
Asārla sār mūkkela jinnen
  Sos gávered 'dré lester zī.

O chūredo kairdas a kúsno
O'· papero, léskro drom :
Sos chitti, āver kennā-sīg
'   Yúv díckdas o bōro Rom :
Pā Mister Ayres, sherréscro,
    Kún háderdas shérro to pen :
" Pūkkerāva man táchodīr lávus
    Shūndes tīro mīraben !

" Tu jāsa fon 'kai to Lúndra,
    Te lódder 'dré yéckli gáv
Te rākker sār Anglatérra,
    Te shūn kékker jāfra láv
Sī o deepodīresto pennis
    Te sī adré Rómmani,
Sī kek but mi-deari Dúvel
    Jinélla 'dúll' láv—te mī."

I pūri dye dicked kālo,
    Te dias o yākk asā,
Sā būti to pen : " Mā pūkker
    Agāl o 'this Górgio ajā !"
But the chúredo dicked at mándy
    To kair sā būt' as I could,
Awer kair o' chúmmeny síkker
    For the pátser o Górgio blood.

Pens Mr Ayres, sherréskro,
  As he mūkkered avrī his dūkk,
" *Gūrniáver's* the láv, mi-rýa,
  An' if tūte can pūkker it, pūkk' ! "
I pūri sávvyed at mándy,
  O chúvveny chúr'do, yúv
Dícked pūtchin 'dré mīri yákkor,
  An' tālé apré the pūv.


" Gūrniáver," pens Ayres, sherréscro ;
  " Gūrniáver's the láv I pen ;
You rýas with lils jins būti,
  But this ain't in your jínaben."
An' we béshed with our shérros tālé,
  Béshed pūkeni táller o bor,
An' never rākkerdom chīchī,
  For the láv had kūried us sār.


Āwer Ayres, sā bōro, sos kūshto,
  Sā yúv rākkerdas mīli : " Sir,
Mándy'll síkker tūkey adóvvo :
  Gūrniáver's a cowcumber ;
For *Gūrni's* a cow 'dré Rom'nis,
  An' *Av*, tūte jins, is come,
An' the dūi kairen cow-comer,
  As síkker as mán's a Rom."

II

Then we hádered our shérros apópli,
   At the bōro lávéngero,
An' ye dye an' sār o' the chávor
   An' the chúr'do an' mán shelled, "*Oh!*"
Kekker shūndom mándy a gúdli
   Sā dūro te bōro.   No.
Penāva te rūkkor te pánni
   Kedívvus shán pūkkerin : "Oh !"

                        CHARLES G. LELAND.

# DOG-GIPSY.

—o—

A Gipsy and a Gentile,
　A grandmother dark and wild,
Five children, and an uncle—
　A half-blood poor and mild.
But the chief was bold and haughty,
　And often declared to me,
That no man in all the country
　Was so deep in their tongue as he.

The crone, a dark old Gipsy,
　Seemed angry to hear me speak;
The half-blood sported a stove-pipe,*
　And I saw that the man was weak.
But the chief looked proudly about him,
　And every motion said
To the world, that all things worth knowing
　Were hidden in *his* great head.

---

* Stove-pipe or chimney-pot; a high hat.

The half-blood was weaving a basket
   Of paper, quietly,
Mere trifling, and as he wove it
   He glanced at the Rommany :
At Mr Ayres the captain,
   Who lifted his head to say :
" I'll tell you the deepest word now
   You ever heard in your day.

" You may go from here to London,
   Wherever our tongue is heard ;
You may talk all England over,
   And never hear sitch a word :
It's the very deeperest *turn*, Sir,
   There is in all Rommany :
There's none but the Lord above us
   As knows o' that word—and me."

The grandmother looked angry,
   And gave him a hurried wink,
As much as to say : "Don't tell it
   Before these Gentiles,—think ! "
But the half-breed gave me another,
   To do the best I could,
But to certainly make an effort,
   For the credit of English blood.

Said Mr Ayres the captain,
　　And his voice came far from below ;
" *Gurniaver's* the word, my master,
　　And if you can explain it—do ! "
The old woman's laugh was scornful,
　　The half-breed glanced around
Up into my eyes, inquiring,
　　Then down upon the ground.


" *Gurniaver,*" said Ayres the captain ;
　　" *Gurniaver's* the word. It's true
You gents with your books knows something,
　　But this here is ahead of you."
So we sat with our heads all bowing,
　　And never a sound was heard ;
And we never uttered a whisper ;
　　We were crushed by that awful word !


But Ayres, though great, was human,
　　So he said politely, " Sir,
This here is wot is the meanin'—
　　*Gūrniáver's* a cow-cumbér :
For a *gūrni's* a cow in Gipsy,
　　And *áv,* you know, is ' come ; '
And the two of 'em make cow-come-r,
　　As certain as I'm a Rom ! "

Then we lifted our heads together
To the linguist—all in a row;
And the grandmother and the children,
And the half-blood and I, cried, "*Oh!*"
I never heard an utterance
So deep and so earnest. No.
I ween that the wood and water
In that dell are still murmuring, "*Oh!*"

CHARLES G. LELAND.

---

This incident, for which I am indebted to a friend, occurred precisely as it is told. It is not unusual for a simple-minded Gipsy to form, after long study, some extraordinary compound of words, or some translation of them from English, on the strength of which invention he patents himself as *deep* Rommany. Sometimes a Gipsy is the possessor of one "deep" word, which he imparts only as a great favour. *Jūkalo Rommanīs*, or Dog-Gipsy, is a term like "Dog-Latin." It is applied to *mis*-applied words. Thus *lel*, signifying to take or get, would become decidedly *jūkalo* if one were to say *lel avrī* for "get out," or *lel up pālī, aprē the wārdo*—"get up behind on the waggon." "*Mandy dūi*" (*i.e.*, I *two*), for I *too*, may be occasionally heard. The Old Professor, so frequently mentioned in "The English Gipsies," on being asked the word for a daisy, suggested that "*Spreadamengrō-adrē-the-sāla-an'-pandamengro-adrē-the-rātti*" would be a very good word—its literal meaning being "A spreading thing (or umbrella) in the morning, and a shutting-up thing at night." My friend, to whom this was said, had suggested that, for want of a better word, *daisy* might be literally translated *dīvvusko yāk*, but the Professor would not hear of this—it lacked the dignity and poetry of his own formidable epithet.

# SÁ O ROMMANY CHAL MŪKKED PĪIN LEVINOR.

———o———

"Mat, hav acai! mā pūr ajā;
 Sār 'shán tu kūshto, pūro pál?
Tu's díckin būti náflo, bā,
 Tu chíndes tīro kālo bál.

"'Kai, pī a cúrro lévinor!"   "Kek—
 Kek, pals kennā; for mandy's káired
A kúrran kek to sūm o' yeck,
 Since mīri poori jūva méred."

"Méred! sār sos 'dóvo?"   "Mándy'll pén,
 O tíkno, mándy, yói té sār
Apré a būti shíllo wén,
 Sos hátched taláy a bōro bor.

"Yói'd lélled a tíkno, té ye báv',
 A wéllin fit ta mōr a mūsh,
Atút ye pūv dūr fon ye gáv,
 Kaired mīri chóri rákli dúsh.

" Yói pendas mándy : ' Deari rom,
  Shom shíllo !   Kair a yāg apré ;
'Dói's būti kóshters 'pré ye drom,
  Sā jā té rikk a bítt' adré.'

" Sā mándy pīrries án, té wells
  Būt sīg apré a kóshter-stogg ;
A bítti kóshter 'dói I léls,
  To káir a kūshtodīrus yāg.

" Mi péndom : ' Jāva man adói
  Ke' 'dóvo kítchema, té kin
A cúrro lévinor for yói ;
  Yói'll kām a droppi hotched, I jin.'

" Āwer a múscro 'pré a gry
  Dicked méngy lel ye kósht, té pénned :
' Tu kālo chor, wūs' lis akái,
  Or tūte'll sīg be stárriben'd ! '

" Adóvo kaired mi húnnalo :
  ' So's tute !  béngis 'dré your zī !
Mūkk méngy jāl, tu dínnelo,
  Or lel your trūppo sīg avrī ! '

" Sā mándy hátched to kūr mī rye ;
  But sīggerdīr as tu could dick
Yuv pūsimegrīed léster gry,
  And wūssered mándy 'dré ye chick.

" Adóvo kaired mé divio, pals,
  Sā mándy lélled a chūri 'vrī,
An' as to látcher mī yúv jāls,
  I kūrs lis sīg at léster zī.

" Āwer yúv délled a pūraben,
  Te mīri chūri pelt aláy ;
Mi sīgaben sos hóckerpen—
  Ye wásterméngris chívved apré.

" Āvo—yúv lélled mī kéti gáv :
  Ye bítcherin-mūshor shūned yúv pén,
Kek mūkked a mándy pen a láv,
  Té bitchered mi ta starripen.

" Pāsh dūi chone yol mūkked mī jā ;
  Āwer yol pénned mī at ye gáv,
Mi-deari jūva, tíkno—sár
  Had mūllered 'dré ye shíllo báv !

" Adóvo póggered mīri zī,
  Vānka man mūkkdom pāsh o bor :
An' sensus mándy kāms to pī
  Kekūmi dróppi lévinor."

                              E. H. Palmer.

# WHY THE GIPSY LEFT OFF
## DRINKING BEER.

———o———

" Mat, come here, lad, don't turn away ;
　　How are you, brother ?　I declare
You're lookin' awful bad to-day ;
　　You've been and cut your long black hair.

" Here, drink a drop o' beer, lad ! "　" No—
　　No thank ye, boys.　I can't abide
The sight o' beer now ; it's been so
　　With me since my poor missus died."

" Died !　How was that ? "　" Well, by your leave,
　　I'll tell you.　I, the babe, and she
Was camping, one cold winter's eve,
　　Against a little blackthorn tree.

" Across the open field the wind
　　Came blowin', fit a'most to kill
A man, and she, but just confined,
　　Poor deary, took a nasty chill.

"Says she to me : 'Matthew, my dear,
  I'm cold ; make up the fire, lad, do !
There's lots o' faggots close by here,
  Just run outside and get a few.'

" So off I goes, and on the road
  I sees some nice dry faggot-ricks ;
And takes from one a little load,
  To make a better fire o' sticks.

" Says I : ' I'll just go over there
  To yonder public-house, and buy
A half-a-pint o' beer for her ;
  She'll like it warmed up by and by.'

" A mounted p'liceman from the town
  Had seen me take the sticks, and so—
' You black thief, throw them faggots down,'
  Says he, ' or off to jail you go ! '

" That made my temper far from cool ;
  ' Curse you ! ' I cried, ' you've got no right
To touch me.   Let me go, you fool !
  Or take off that there coat and fight ! '

" And I stood up to fight, of course ;
  But quicker than a wink, he rode
Straight at me, spurrin' of his horse,
  And knocked me over on the road.

"That only made me twice as mad ;
  So out I pulls my pocket-knife,
And as he come to seize me, lad,
  I struck at him, to take his life.

"He gave a sudden turn—I stopped,
  And saw at once that I had missed
My chance that time ; my knife had dropped :
  The handcuffs were upon my wrist.

"Yes, off he took me to the jail !
  The beaks heard what *he'd* got to say.
But wouldn't let me tell my tale,
  And locked me up, right straight away.

"In two months' time they let me go ;
  But in the village I was told,
My babe, the wife that loved me so,
  Had died that same night in the cold.

"My heart was broken by that there,
  For those I'd lost, and loved so dear :
And now you know why I don't care
  To touch another drop o' beer."

E. H. PALMER.

It should be stated in explanation of this poem that Gipsies
reverence their dead by abstaining from some favourite food,

amusement, or habit. This is generally connected in some way with the deceased. Thus, a Gipsy having smoked a pipe with a friend the last time he met him, and before his death, will, *in memoriam*, refrain from tobacco for several years. (See "The English Gipsies and their Language," chap. iv. Trübner & Co., 1873.)

## O KUSHTO DŪKKERIN.

—o—

"Kai sos tu, mīro kāmlo,
  Avéssa sā ráttescri ?—
Te kai sos tu, mī tácho kāmlo,
  Tīro wongur's sār náshered avrī ? "

" Shómas 'drín o wésh, mīri kāmli,
  Kai sar i chíriclor gill,
Kai o bítti rūkkéngro hóckers,
  Kai i tāni kūkalos kill.

" Sos a Rómmani dye adói,
  Sār kāli sims o wen :
Yói díckdas 'dré mīri wástor,
  Te pūkkerdas dūkkerben.

" Yói péndas mi rúmmav' a rāni,
  Sār safráni bályor,
Sār rínkeni nīli yakkor,
  Te chámor sim rūzhior."

"Mīri yākkor shán sār nili,
Mīri balyor shán safrán "——
"Lis mūkkdas lovva, mī kāmli,
Shūnáv tu rúméssa mán."

JANET TUCKEY.

————o————

" WHERE have you been, my darling,
　　That you come so late at night ?—
And where have you been, my own love,
　　That your purse has grown so light ?"

" I have been in the forest, darling ;
　　I have heard the wood birds sing,
Where the squirrel picked nuts for the winter,
　　And the fairies had made a ring.

" A Gipsy came through the forest ;
　　She was wrinkled, brown, and old ;
And she looked in my hand, and I listened
　　To the fortune that she told.

" She told me I soon should marry
　　A lady with yellow hair—
A lady with flower-blue eyes, love,
　　And cheeks like the wild-rose fair."

" *My* hair is yellow as sunshine,
  My eyes are violet-blue "——
" Ah ! wasn't it worth the money
  To hear that I'll marry *you ?* "

JANET TUCKEY.

SHŪN the húnnalo o' the pánni,
  The húnnalo bōro pánni,
  Húnnalin sārasā',
  'Cos it can't jāl andūro,
  An' gūryin ajā !

M. C.

HEAR the roar of the water,
  Of the great and raging sea,
  Raging ever'on,
  Because it can get no further,
  And roaring all alone !*

C. G. L.

---

* The Rommany original of these lines was the utterance of a tent-Gipsy on being asked what was his word for " roar." There is a double meaning in it, since *hunnalo* also signifies rage.

## MŪLLO BÁLOR.

——o——

Oh ! I jässed to the kér,
  An' I tried to māng the bālor ;
Tried to māng the mūllo bālor,
  When I jässed to the kér.

But the rāni wouldn't del it,
  For she pénnas les 'os drábberd,
For she pénnas les 'os drábberd,
  Penn's the Rómmany chál had drábbed the
    bālor.

M. C.

# DEAD PIG.

———o———

I WENT to the farmhouse
Where I knew a pig had died,
And to get it I emplored 'em
Till I pretty nearly cried.

But the lady wouldn't give it,
And she 'inted rather free
As 'twas pisoned by some Gipsy,
And that Gipsy man was *me*.

CHARLES G. LELAND.

This trifle, which I heard sung by a Gipsy in Brighton, will recall to many readers the ballad in Mr Borrow's " Rommany Rye." It is said that poisoning pigs for the sake of feeding on their flesh is no longer practised ; but I venture to assert, with some confidence, that it is by no means one of the lost arts, and that a weakness for *mullo baulor*, or pork which died by " the hand of God " (or by disease), as the Continental Gipsies say, is certainly not one of the lost tastes, as I doubt whether there is a real Gipsy, old or young, in England who has not eaten it. This is a subject which has, however, never been really understood, and it is a gross injustice to base on it an indiscriminate appetite for refuse food of any kind. No Gipsy would touch horse-flesh, and I have known one who professed a fondness for *mullo baulor*, but did not like anchovy paste and similar dainties. Thus, the Chippeway Indians, who have some eccentric fancies as to food, do not like oysters, though truth compels me to admit that one among them whom I once met went far in the opposite direction. When camping in the wilderness in 1868, at the western extremity of Lake Superior, I sent a tin of oysters to a dozen Indians who were eating their dinner at a little distance from where I was seated with my friends. The open canister, containing a quart of the shell-fish, was gravely passed from one to the other without examination or comment, until it came to the last man, who as gravely lifted it to his mouth, and, almost without a pause, *drank off* the entire contents to the last oyster, and with it all the liquid. On asking some explanation of this extraordinary proceeding, I was simply told, "Him likee um oyster." There was something very Gipsy-like in the grave manner in which this was done, and I find myself continually detecting a great similarity in the Rommany saying and doing of many strange things, common to Indians, Gipsies, and Negroes, which it would be extremely difficult to explain or even set forth to a " Gorgio."

As to *mullo baulor*, the taste is traditional. There is a very large caste or class of outcasts in India, whose names, Dom and Domni, strongly suggest Rom and Romni, who are probably *in part* ancestors of the European Gipsies. These Doms, who are wanderers like Gipsies, resemble them in the peculiarity of eating " dead " animals, particularly pigs. The Doms also carry out corpses, flay beasts, and exercise other functions, all of which were for centuries peculiar to the Roms in Europe, and which have remained their specialty to the present generation in Denmark.* In all the countries in which they have lived, nothing has ever been so characteristic of the Roms as this fancy for *mullo baulor*—nothing has tended more to separate them from Gorgios in popular prejudice, and there is nothing to which they have adhered with greater obstinacy. One reason for this is unquestionably the fact that *mullo baulor* is extremely agreeable to Gipsy palates. I have never eaten it myself, but I have eaten hedgehog, which is really very nice, being tender, with a flavour like pheasant; and Gipsies have assured me that it is precisely like *mullo baulor*, and hardly to be distinguished from it. Another Rommany excuse for such food is that it is wholesome, and that no one was ever yet made ill by eating it, which is certainly more than can be said of the best of game with a *haut gout*. It is, however, more than probable that *mullo baulor*, which produces no evil effect on a Gipsy, who lives in the open air, and who is constantly exercising, would half-poison a kérengro, or house-dweller. All Gipsies who have eaten *mullo baulor* persist that it tastes better than any other food whatever; and I am quite convinced that they feel a certain pride in being emancipated from a prejudice to which "Gorgios" are enslaved. I have very little doubt that the legends of ghouls, which are simply the supernatural form of the Aghora (or Ogre) sect in India, sprung from the extravagant emancipation from all "prejudice" which was developed by advanced thinkers among Hindu sages; and it is not entirely impossible that both Eastern and Western cynicism have their origin in this Oriental source. It may yet be found that the orthodox Oriental prohibition of pork as food involved more than is now known, and that it was truly a *pièce de résistance* between

---

* *Vide* Tatere og Natmandsfolk i Danmark. Af F. Dyrlund. Kopenhagen, F. Hegel, 1872.

the ultra-emancipationists of early ages and the "Con-servatives," so to speak.  Christianity, so progressive in many respects, avoided this degree of Radicalism, if we may judge by the significant miracle of the driving of the herd of swine into the sea.  It is tolerably apparent that, from the earliest Egyptian times, the wild boar or pig was identified with the evil principle, just as the emanci-pated or Free Thinkers have been, very naturally indeed, by the Orthodox ; and it may be that while those who dared to eat pork which had been butchered were simply wicked, those who went a step further, and ate *mullo baulor* on prin-ciple, were "damnable."  More than one of the mysterious sects of heretics in the Middle Ages had the pig for a symbol. It would be curious to know if eating pork ever formed a charge against the Knights Templars.  The reader will excuse the length of these very speculative remarks, should he deem it possible that there exists in England a class whose persistency in such unnatural diet was *partially* derived from early Indian illumination.

——o——

TUTE'S shūned o Róммany drom, shaián,
Ta pen sor religionus hóckerpen ;
But I jins ke rasháior sor tácheni shan,
For mī dickdom o béng adrè a tan,
Yck dívvus, sār mínno yäckerpen.

Mándy hátcherdum 'pré a póv,
Arāti, talé yeck bōro rūkh ;
Āwer mándy nástis jínned sār to sōv,
Te chúmmany 'drè mī ánkaired to róv,
"Tīro bítti mýla sī wélled to dūkh."

Pendum mándy, "mūks dick avrī ;"
Sā avrī adrè o báv I wells,
Te odói in the rāti, āvalí !
Hatchélla o mýla, te kūshto sī,
Te lésker hābben o' pūs yúv lélls.

" Hávacái," mī rākk'dom, táchipen,
Mendūi shómas kūshti páls,

Yuv'd práster aprè at my shūnaben,
Chiv his nāk in my vást, till tūte'd pen
'Dóvo mýla sos yéck o' de Rómmany cháls.

Āwer 'dóvo chīrus—mī kek jins sār,—
Āwer jindom kūshto the trásh I lélled—
Hātchélla pūkkeno síms a bár,
Āwer jālled andūro sārasār,
The dūrodīrus te mándy wélled.

Te pāl' a bittus yúv yūzhered avrī,
Te the sāla jíndom the táchipen,
Dóvo slómmado mýla sī hóckeny,—
O pūro bengs nōko kókero sī;
Te mínno sos chído dré pánderpen.

Kávakai's kek tácho te fóki pen,
Ké sār o' de chóvveny Rómmany cháls
Shan Dúvvel-násherdo wáffodipen;
For o Bengis avélla a dūrriken len,
Pénsi kéti sār wāvior fóki—pals!

E. H. PALMER.

# SMITH AND THE DEVIL.

MEBBE you've heard it's the Rommany way
To say that religion is lies ;
But I know it's all true what the parsons say,
For I saw the Devil myself one day,
With these 'ere blessed eyes.

I was campin' out on a field one night,
But I couldn't sleep a wink ;
For I suddenly got a sort of a fright,
And I fancied the donkey warn't all right,—
Now 'twas prophecy, that, I think.

Then I says, "I'll take a look around,"
So out in the air I went ;
And there in the dim half-light I found
That the donkey was standin' safe and sound,
A-grazin' outside the tent.

"Come hup !" I says, says I, to the moke,
For him and me was friends ;

An' he allus knew me when I spoke,
An' he úsed to canter up and poke
His nose into my hands.

But this 'ere time, and I needn't say
That I thought it rather rum,
Though he stood as still as a lump of clay,
Yet the furder he seemed to get away
The nigher I tried to come.

At last he wanished out of sight,
And I knew, when day came round,
That the donkey I'd followed all through the night
Was the Devil himself,—for when 'twas light
I saw my own in the pound.

It's a wrong idea most folks have got,
That Rommany chaps like me
Haven't any dear God to look after the lot;
For the Devil he tempts us quite as hot
As any one else, you see.

                                    E. H. PALMER.

This story was told by a Gipsy in Suffolk, who firmly
believed, like the rustic in the old Joe Miller story, that he
had actually seen the Devil or a ghost in the likeness of a
"great ass."

# SĀ LIS JÍNSA TU?

—o—

"Oh, jínsa tu, mī chávi, sā rínkeni tūte shán?"

"Āvo, ávali, mīri dye?"

"Āwer sī kek dickaméngro 'dré mōro bítti tán,

Sā jínsa tūte lis, mīri chi?"

"I fóki 'pré o dróm,

O Górgio te o Róm,

Shán sīg ta pūkker mándy sā rínkeni mi shom."

"'Dré sávo jíb, mī chávi, pūkkelan i fóki lis?

Mā pen méngy hockaben, mī chi!

Rākker yúl Górgiones or tácho Rómmanis?"

"Oh, yúl násti rākker chīchī, mīri dye;

Yúl sósti pen kek láv,

Āwer díck ajā te sáv,

Te jināva shom i kāmlidīri jūva 'dré o gáv!"

JANET TUCKEY.

# HOW DO YOU KNOW IT?

—o—

"OH, do you know, my daughter, that you've a pretty
 face?"
"Surely, and surely, mother mine!"
"But see, there's no mirror, not one in all the place,
 So how do you know it, daughter mine?"
  "Oh, up the road and down,
  The fair folk and the brown,
They tell me there's no beauty like myself in all the
 town."

"And how do they talk to you?—make haste to answer
 this—
And tell me no fibs, daughter mine;
Do they speak the Gorgio language, or good old Rom-
 manis?"
  "Oh, they needn't say a word, mother mine;
  They need only smile so bland,
  And I'm quick to understand
There isn't such a beauty as myself in all the land!".
        JANET TUCKEY.

I TĀNI múllos 'pré o dóeyav
Shan sār i sāni chūmer o' the báv ;
O lūllopen apré i pábor chám
Li sī i tátti chūmer o' the kám ;
Te 'dóvo rínkeni dipplor tīri mūi
Shán mīri chūmer, oh, mi kāmelí !

— ..

THE little bubbles floating on the wave
Are all soft kisses which the west wind gave ;
The luscious glow upon the peach's face
Bears blushing witness to the sun's embrace ;
And those two dimples, Sweet, that come and go,
Tell tales of true-love kisses—is it so ?

# I CHIRIKI.

—o—

" Pūro pál, pen yéckcovva améngy,
Pūkka Rommanescro *stars* 'dré chīrus ? "
" Āvo, rýa.   Stárya shan shīrkīs,
Dóvo láv fon chīricli avélla.
Chīricli shūnélla pensi shírkī ;
Te i shírk'li shán sār dūdni chírcli :
Pā yúl mūkkeran dūro práller shérro.
Yāgni chíriclór arātti jána
Te o chone sī rāni o' the chīrus.
Yói avélla sīg jinés' sārrāti
'Pré o pūv ta póller lākis kánnis."

Charles G. Leland.

# THE STARS.

—-o—

" TELL me this, old friend, if you can tell it,
What's the Rommany for *stars* in heaven ? "
" Yes, my master.   Stars with us are *shīrkis,*
And from *chīriclis* or birds, I take it.
For the birds and stars are like in nature :
Stars are only birds of light in heaven,
Flying far above our heads for ever ;
Birds of fire which only fly in darkness :
And the moon's the lady of the heavens,
Coming nightly, certain in her coming,
O'er the meadow, just to feed her chickens."

CHARLES G. LELAND.

---

*Chirki,* or *shirki,* a star in Rommany, may possibly have something in common with the Persian *chirkh,* meaning the sky, or *chiragh,* a lamp.

The idea here expressed is given very nearly in the words of an old Gipsy.

# I PŪRI RÓMMANY DYE'S DŪI CHÁVIOR.

—o—

JÁSSIN yek dívvus adré a gáv,
  A 'chóvvany bitti kér I látched,
Te a pūri Rómmany, Bunce by náv
  Akónya 'drè adóvo hátched.

" Sār'shán tu," péndum, " pūri dye ? "
  Te my stárdy leldum shérro avrī ;
(Tu sásti kéravit sims a rye,
  Kāméssa tu rūkker 'dré Rómmany).

" Sóssi," pútched mándy, " deari dye,
  A dye sims tūte kairéngri shán ?
Kai's tūte mūkkered your fóki, kai ?
  Te kai tu chīdas o bítti tán ? "

" Ah ! a chóvveny jūva mándy shom,
  Sor akónya 'drè pūripen I jiv ;
Būti chīrus náshcrdum miro rom,
  Te as for tánya, I've kek to chiv.

"Āwer dūi chávior mándy lells,
   Yek o' léndy's rúmmor'd a Górgiko mūsh ;
Ah ! rýa, to waffódipén she wélls,
   For the rátfelo Górgio kairs her dúsh.

" Kek kāmāva lāti sā būti ajā,
   Tho' her wáffody jívvin it kairs me róv ;
Āwer yék so kāmāva i kūshtidir,
   Sovélla adrè o kángri póv."

E. H. PALMER.

K

# THE OLD WOMAN'S TWO DAUGHTERS.

———o———

WALKING about in a village, I came
  On a wretched little hovel once,
Where was living a lonely Gipsy dame,
  Who went by the name of Phœbe Bunce.

" How are you, mother ? "  And as I spoke
  I lifted my hat from off my head ;
(If you want to talk to Gipsy folk,
  You must act like a gentleman born and bred).

" My dear old lady," I asked, " how's this ?
  A house isn't surely the place for you ;
Where have you left your folk ?  I miss
  Your tent ; why, where have you put that to ? "

" I'm a poor old woman, and all alone
  I live in my old age as you see ;
I lost my husband long years agone,
  And as for tents, there is none for me.

" But two dear daughters I still have got,
  One of 'em's married an English lad ;
Ah, sir ! but hers is a hard, hard lot,
  For the wretched fellow he treats her bad.

" The love as I bears to her is small,
  Though to think of her sorrow I often weeps ;
But the one as I loves the best of all,
  In a lonely churchyard, sir, she sleeps."

E. H. PALMER.

The above conversation, recalling " We are Seven," is given
nearly as it was carried on between an old Gipsy woman
and a friend of the writer.

# LEL RĀKı

———o———

Lᴇʟ rāk, pal—hatch apré !
Jāl i graiya—práster—
Práster pā tīro míraben !
O rye avélla, táchipen,
Tu lūrdas o graia kāliko ;
Te vel yúv dícksa tūte,
Yúv shéllela avrī tālla yākengro,
Te bitcherav tūte ke stáripen.
Lel vin, lel trád !

J. T.

———

Lᴏᴏᴋ sharp, brother—hurry away !
Run the horses !  Run—
Run for your life !  I'm telling you true,
The farmer's coming—the one
You stole the horse from yesterday ;
And if he gets a glimpse of you,
He'll call the police, and then the beak
Will keep you in jail for many a week.
Take care !  beware !

J. T.

# MĪRI KĀMELI PĪRRÝNI.

——o——

JINĀVA mé o tácho náv
Kūshtiko cóvvar adré o gáv
Āver kūshtidīro a méngi zī
Sī mīri kāmeli pīrrýni.

Béshāva sārdívvus adrín o tán,
Penāva i fóki, "Sarishán :"—
Āver béshāva bésh, ta díckāv o mūi
O' mīri kāmeli pīrrýni.

Kāmāva te vél a bōro rye ;
Kāmāva ta lél a kūshto gry :
Āver wūsserāva i dūi avrī,
To chūmer mī kāmeli pīrrýni.

CHARLES G. LELAND.

# THE GIRL WHO LOVES ME WELL.

———o———

I CAN tell you the name right down
Of the prettiest things in all the town ;
But there isn't a thing the people sell
So fine as the girl who loves me well.

I sit in my Gipsy tent all day,
And, " How are you all ? " to the folk I say ;
But I'd sit for a year, and it's truth I tell,
For a glimpse of the girl who loves me well.

Oh, I'd like to be a lord, of course,
And I'd like to have a hunting-horse ;
But the one and the other I'd gladly sell,
For a kiss from the girl who loves me well.

CHARLES G. LELAND.

---

This ballad is founded on no especial incident, but may be
set down as Rommany, having met with a cordial reception
among tent-Gipsies.

# ROMMANY JINABEN.

———o———

APRÉ a rātti 'dré a shíllo wen
Yāg poggerélla 'vrī adré a kér,
Ye mūshor sār for léngeris mīrabeu
Práster, te kékkeno jīns sā ta kair :
Yeck rīkk'la páni, te a wāver shells :
" Hūker ye cóvvus sār apré ye pūv ! "
Ye grūvni gūjers te i grásni dells ;
Ye bitti tíknos te i jūvas rúvv.
Āwer a chóvveni Rómmany jūva wells,
An' hátchin pāsh o ye yāgescro chib,
Hótchélla wástor, penla Róm'ny jib :
" A yāg's a kūshti cóvva 'dré o wen,
Yeck's wāfro bāk sī wāvior's kāmmaben."

E. H. PALMER.

# GIPSY PHILOSOPHY.

———o———

ONE wintry night, upon a certain farm,
A fire broke out; the folks in great alarm,
Not knowing what to do, all run about.
Some bring up water, others only shout:
"Fetch out the things into the field here, quick!"
The oxen bellow, and the horses kick;
The little children and the women cry;
But a poor Gipsy who was passing by
Stood near the flames that from the building sprung,
And warmed her hands, and said in Gipsy tongue:
"A fire in winter does one good to see;
What's your bad luck may prove good luck to me!"

E. H. PALMER.

# FRANK COOPER.

—o—

A LÓRDUS vias kéti wélgóro—
   Rýa te rāniya shan bárveli :
A tāno rye te a kāmelo—
   Āvo, mi pīrrynī, āvali !

O rye yúv díckdas Frank Cooper adói :
   Āvo, mi pīrrynī, āvali !
Sār būti dūdeni pīvlIói
   For lórdis an' swélli sā bārveli.

O lórdus shūndas mi Rómmani pén,
   " Well án, mi rýor sā bārveli !
Sīg 'dústa you lel your lóvvy again
   If you'il wūsser my kóshters, āvali.

" Dick at the sīggabens, rýa, dick—
   Dick at the nútti, āvali,
Hátchin alángus sār of a rikk,
   Hátchin' for rýor sā bārveli.

"Trin kóshters a hórra shán kávacói,
    O bávol pūdela, āvali,
Kūshto ta dél at the pīvliói—
Kūshto for rýor sā bārveli.

"Yeck núttus beshólla 'pré léster kósh,
    Sávvyin, sālerin, āvali!
But kennā-sīg tūte vel kérelen dūsh,
    An' mūller the monkeys, dóvali.

"Rýas chávor, pīrri akái,
    Kennā sī o chánsus, āvali!
Lel o' mī kóshters, kūshto rye
    Sī pyáss for fóki sā bārveli."

O rye las Cooper's kóshter adói,
    Būt adústa, sā rýor bārveli,
Te wūssered adróm at the pīvliói,
    Te lélldas a būtus, āvali.

But when pāsh o' the pīvliói sos mōred
    An the rye had lélled akóva-li,
Yúv látched his bōro chúkko was chóred,
    Sā yúv sas a-wūsserin—āvali.

A bōro chúkko te twenty bár :
    For the rye sos yeck o' the bārveli ;
An' his pāni wásteni te sār,
    Násho te jíllo, āvali.

Pūkkerdas rye o Rómmani chál :
   "Mīro chúkko sī chóredo, āvali !
An' tūte a-hátchin just ánerjāl—
   Sā pénnas tūte o' dóvali ?

"If fóki sos lódderin mīro kér,
   Chóreni fóki or bárveli,
'Fore I'd mūkk 'em be lūredo I'd sīgger mér,
   An' túte's a Rómmani, āvali !"

Frank Cooper sī pórdo o' kālo rātt,
   As sāno as yeck kekāva-li,
But wélled as pāno as if he were skāt,
   To shūn o' the rýa, āvali.

Frank Cooper's a mūsh ké sī búnnalo,
   Yúv'll kékker kéravit wāver-li ;
An' the béng never dícked more húnnalo
   Than Frank when he shūnavit, āvali.

Yúv hátched a sīggus pūkkenus,
   Te shūned o' the rýas láva-li ;
Then prástered avrī sims dívius,
   'Dré the sīg o' the mūshor, āvali.

The rye never dūkkered his kókero,
   For yúv sos yéck o' the bárveli,
An' pátsered the Cooper tácheno,
   So yúv rākkered Alisa, āvali.

Till the Rómmani chál vias pāladói,
    Yuv béshcd an' shūned lākis láva-li ;
When apópli to léster pīvlnői
    Frank wélled with the chúkko, āvali.

Yéck o' léstis yākkor sós kālo ajā,
    An' the wāver wasn't wāver-li,
As if yúv'd dícked the béng te sā
    Since yúv dícktav the rýa, āvali.

" 'Kai's tīro wóngur, mi rye," péns he,
    " 'Kai's the lóvvy sā bārveli ;
'Kai shán i pāni wásteni—
    Dick if it's tácho, āvali !

" Mándy's tūkno o' hátchin sā longadūr,
    Āwcr man nasti kéravit wāvcr-li,
For with kūroméscros a mūsh must kūr,
    An' I had ta kūr for it—āvali ! "

O rýc lélled lésters pūtsi avrī,
    An' látchcd the wóngur sā bārveli,
An' délled pánj bár to the Rómmani,
    As a ryc should kéravit, āvali.

An' if tūtc'll jāl to the pīvlnői
    At the Epsom prásterin, wāvcr-li,
Tūtc can dick Frank Cooper adói
    An' Alis yúvs jūva, āvali.

Sī tūte kāméss' müttermóngerī,
  You can lél it fon léns kekāvi-li,
An' if Alis the jūva isn't avrī,
  Yói'll dŭkker your rāṇi—āvali!

CHARLES G. LELAND.

# FRANK COOPER.

——o——

A LORD he went to the fair one day,
   Oh, lords are rich, and their ladies too !
A little lord, and his heart was gay,
   Yes, my darling, I tell you true.

The lord he saw Frank Cooper there ;
   Yes, my darling, I tell you true !
With a lot of cocoa-nuts at the fair,
   All for lords and gentlemen too.

The lord he heard Frank Cooper shout :
   " Come, noble gents, here's the game for you :
You'll win back your money, you needn't doubt,
   If you throw these here sticks, I tell you true.

" Look what a chance, my noblemen, see !
   Look at the nuts, don't I tell you true ?
All along in a row they be,
   Waiting for gentlemen just like you.

" Three sticks a penny, my lords, look here !
   And the wind's a blowin' just right for you ;
You'll hit the cocoa-nuts, never fear,
   And win the lot—don't I tell you true ?

" Every cocoa-nut's on its stick—
   So pert—why, they might be laughin' at you !
But take a throw, and they'll fall so quick,
   And you'll kill the monkeys, I tell you true.

" Gentlemen's sons, won't you step this way ?
   Here is your chance, I tell you true ;
Come, take hold of the sticks and play—
   This is the game for swells like you."

The lord took twenty or thereabouts—
   Took a lot, as gentlemen do,
And he fired away at the cocoa-nuts,
   And punished them well, I tell you true.

But when half the nuts were tumbled down—
   With so clever a hand the gentleman threw—
He found that his overcoat was gone,
   So he left off playing—ay, that is true.

A beautiful coat and twenty pound—
   The lord was rich and the coat was new—
And his light kid gloves he'd thrown on the ground,
   All of 'em stolen—I tell you true.

The lord he said : " Why, this is too bad!
My coat is stolen, I tell you true ;
And you were near it, my Gipsy lad—
Where's the thief, and what shall I do ?

" If I had a guest," the lord he said,
" Rich like myself or poor like you,
'Fore I'd see him robbed I'd sooner be dead,
And you're a Gipsy—ay, that is true ! "

Frank Cooper's blood is as dark as night,
As black as the pot in which Gipsies stew ;
But you'd think he was shot, he grew so white
When he heard the lord—yes, I tell you true.

Frank Cooper's as proud as proud can be,
As proud as the devil and all his crew ;
And never looked devil more fierce than he
When he heard the gentleman—ay, that's true.

He said not a word, the Gipsy man,
But stopped and heard the gentleman through ;
And then, as if he was mad, he ran
Where the crowd was thickest, I tell you true.

The lord didn't trouble himself a bit—
He was one of the rich, and they are few ;
He trusted the Rommani, as was fit,
And talked to Alice, as gentlemen do.

He sat him down by her side, and then
　　He let her chatter, as Gipsies do,
Till Frank came back to the nuts again,
　　Bringing the great-coat as good as new.

One of his eyes was as black as coal,
　　And its fellow was much the same colour too ;
As if he'd seen the devil and all
　　Since he left the lord—yes, I tell you true.

" Here's the money, my lord," said he,
　　" Here's your money all safe for you ;
And the fine white gloves, why, here they be—
　　Look if they're right—have I told you true ?

" I'm sorry that you've been kept waiting so,
　　But I came as fast as a man could do ;
For with fighting chaps one must fight, you know,
　　And I had to fight for it, that is true."

The lord he took his purse from the coat,
　　And found his money all right and true ;
And he gave the Gipsy a five-pound note—
　　Gave it so free, as a lord should do.

Now if you go to the Epsom race,
　　You'll see Frank Cooper, I promise you,
With all his cocoa-nuts in their place,
　　And Alice, his wife, I tell you true.

L

And if you wish for a cup of tea,
They'll boil the kettle and give it you ;
And if Alice is there, your lady'll see
She'll tell her fortune, and tell it true.

JANET TUCKEY.

The story of Frank Cooper was told me, not by the Gipsy himself, but by a gentleman who was present at the occurrence described in the ballad. As the affair was very much to Frank's credit, I have not hesitated to give his name. It may be observed that, for the sake of the rhyme, I have taken a liberty not uncommon in ballads of a humble class, in extending *láv* (a word) to *lávali*, *wáver* (other) to *wáverli*, and *kekávi* (kettle) to *kekávali*. For the information of those readers who do not know what the game of cocoa-nuts, or a cocoa-nut cock-shy, may be, I would explain that stout sticks, about four feet long, are stuck either into the ground or into coarse baskets of matting filled with earth. These are placed in a row, about four feet apart, and behind them at a little distance there is a screen of canvas. On the end of each stick a small cocoa-nut rests, not fastened, but simply balanced. The player hires from the proprietor of the game a bundle of short sticks, about two feet in length, for which he pays a halfpenny each, more or less according to the bargain driven and the quantity taken. He then places himself about twenty-five feet from the stakes, and throws, his object being to displace the cocoa-nuts, which become his property when he can knock them off. ' The canvas screen is indispensable to prevent the sticks from inflicting injury beyond the limits of the play. It is, of course, a rough game, and very dangerous for the Gipsy attendants, who, however, far from avoiding the sticks, often put themselves in the way of receiving serious injuries, hoping to get a present from the thrower. Their indifference to such hurts is very remarkable. I have seen Frank Cooper with a long and deep cut across his head, hastily bound up, playing away in a few minutes, and crying out the characteristic phrases embodied in the ballad, as if nothing had happened. I may add, with regard to cocoa-nuts, the Gipsies believe, or pretend to believe, that one given by them as a present brings that *luck* which they are always bestowing so freely on others, but of which they have so little themselves, as Callot observed long ago.

# DŪKKERIN.

——o——

Chiv a tāni bit o sónaki lóvo
Adré the vást o' de Rómmany dye ;
An' I'll pen yer a dūkkeripen, my rāni—
The kūshtiest ever I pénned a chi.

There's a kūshko pāno rye as kāms you,
An' tūte kāmessa lés tácho ajā ;
An' 'dóis a wāver, a kālo geero,
Mérin for tīro kām kennā.

Te tūte'll rúmmer the pīrreno yók, chi,
An' a táchi rómni'll tūte kér ;
Te tūte'll be dye o' dūi chávyor,
Te jív adré kūshkipen till you mér.

An' if mán'y jins so the stāror pūkker,
To-dívvus'll ríggur you kétteni.—
Dórdi ! akai's a rye a wéllin
That jins my dūkkerin tácho sī !

Mūkk méngy dūkker your kók'ro, rýa—
So? máudy can't pen lis !—mándy can.
Mā tūte sáv' at dūkkerin pāla—
For dóvo sos sār the tem began !

E. H. PALMER.

———o———

CROSS the poor old Gipsy's hand now
With a little bit of gold :
You've the best of luck, my lady,
That the stars have ever told.

There's a fair young man as loves you,
And you love him fond and true ;
There's a dark young fellow also,
Dyin' all for love of you.

And you'll marry him you love, miss,
And you'll make a first-rate wife ;
You'll be mother of two children,
And be happy all your life.

And if I can read the stars right,
You will meet him here to-day—
Look ! here's some one just a comin'
As will bear out all I say.

Shall I tell your fortune too, sir ?
What ? I can't !—Oh, yes I can.
Don't you laugh at fortune-telling :
'Twas with that the world began !

E. H. PALMER.

Sī mīri chūmya shan kūshti to hā,
Tu násti hatch bóckalo, déari, ajā !

IF kisses of mine were good to eat,
You shouldn't go hungry long, my sweet !

———o———

As mándy was pirryin 'pré the dróm,
I dicked the pátteran of a Róm,
Of a Rómmany chál as I did know ;
And the náv o' the músh 'us Petúlengró.

And longo dūro did mándy jéss,
Till I wélled to the yāg where yúv did besh ;
And he pens me " Sārishán ? "—" How do you do ? "
For a tácho Róm was Petúlengró.

" What bāk ta-dívvus ? " I pens, an' he
Pens " Wáfodo bāk " ajā to me.
" It's wáfro bāk wherever I goes,
An' all alángs o' them gavéngroes.

" If I lells a kóshter fon a bár,
There wells ta méngy a hóppercore.
And it's bāk if I ain't starméskeró
Along o' addúvel gavéngeró.

"If mándy's adré in my tan aláy,
An' a bālor wells ān the drúm apré ;
Yuv chivs me avrī, so out I goes,
For it allers jā! with them gávengróes.

"If my jūva jāls to a kér, you jin,
A pénnin a bítto dūkkerin,
Yói's trásherdo mūllo the fust she knows,
Aláng o' them béngalo gávengróes.

"I shūns a gecro rākker to me :
As akóvo's a tem o' liberty,
But I pens the liberty mándy stows,
Is a tem where there's kék o' them gávengróes.

"Oh, I've lélled adústa o'kóvvo tem,
With its ryes and ráshis an' sitch as them ;
An' its párl the páni 'fore lángs I goes,
To a tem where there isn't no gávengróes.

"Adóvo's the tem for a dūkkerin ;
Adóvo's the tem for dūdikabin ;
Kai you jāls as pīrr' as the bávol blows—
Hespesherly from them gávengróes.

"The 'Mericanéskro tem, my pál :
Adóvo's the tem for a Rómmany chál.
For fon sār I shūn, an' fon sār I knows,
They don't késsur adói for no gávengróes."

CHARLES G. LELAND.

———o———

As I was going along the way,
I saw the tracks where a Gipsy lay—
Of a Gipsy fellow whom I did know,
And the name of the man was Petulengro.

And so I went on the road a bit,
Till I came to the fire where I saw him sit;
And he said to me, "Sarishan?"—"How do you do?"
For a real Rom was Petulengro.

"What luck for the day?" I asked, and he
Said, "Wery bad luck," again to me;
"It's wery bad luck, that never will cease,
And all along o' these here police.

"If I pulls a bit of a stick from a hedge,
There's a bobby a bobbin' along its edge;
An' it's luck if I ain't in prison a piece,
An' all along o' that 'ere police.

"When I'm sound asleep in our little camp,
The Pigs come down an' they make us tramp;

They roots me out, and I gets no peace ;
For it's allers 'Move on !' with them 'ere police.

" If my missus gets in a house, you know,
To tell a bit of a fortin' or so,
They scares her almost to her de-cease,
For they're nat'ral devils, is them police.

" I heard a fellow preachin' to me,
As this is the land o' liberty :
But I tells him my liberty is peace ;
An' there's none o' that there, where you has police.

" Oh, I've had enough o' this land, I say,
With its lords and parsons an' sitch as they ;
An' it's over the water I goes like geese,
To a land where there isn't no police.

" There you can tell a fortin' or so ;
There you can clear out the things, you know ;
There you are free as the blowin' breeze :—
Hespesherly from them vile police.

" The 'Merican land, I thinks, mayhap,
Is just the spot for a Rommany chap ;
For from all I hears, there they lives at peace,
An' the people don't care for no police.

CHARLES G. LELAND.

This ballad was partly written one day while associating
with Gipsies, and was drawn from their own remarks.

# ROMMANIS LEL SĀR.

——o——

O KRÁL-RŪKK kāmela dóeyav for léster pīrrynī,
Yói'll kékker dick nor shūn a láv, yoi pells sā sīg avrī.

O Róm keréla lester tán adré o rūkkor lock—
Lels pánni fon i dóeyav, te kóshters fon o shock.

A bōro Górgio kāms a chi for léster rōmeli,
Āwer yói'll kékker shūn o rye, sā jūla sīg avrī.

"Sā jinsa tu adóvo, mi pūri kāli dye?"
Oh, mándy dūkkered sāridūi, i rāni te o rye.

Avéllan yéck akónyo, ī rāni te o rye,
Te sāridūi dés méngy sā būti sónnakai.

O bōro rūkk, i dóeyav, o mūsh so kāmela,
I dínneli jūva,—Rómmanis lel kūshto bāk fon sā.

JANET TUCKEY.

## ALL IS FISH TO THE GIPSY NET.

———o———

AN oak-tree loves a rivulet, but she will never stay
To look at him or hear a word, she runs so fast away.

And there beneath the forest boughs the Rommanis are free
To take the water from the brook and firewood from
    the tree.

There's a lord that loves a lady, and she will never stay
To hear him when he speaks of love, but lightly trips
    away.

"My Gipsy mother, can you tell how all of this was
    known ? "
The lord and lady came to me, and each of them alone ;

They came to me so secretly and crossed my hand with
    gold,
They sat inside the Gipsy tent, and had their fortune told.

From the lover and his lady, from rivulet and tree,
From all of them we help ourselves, for we are Rommani.

JANET TUCKEY.

# CHARLIE O RÁSHIMÉNGRO.

—o—

I AIN'T lelled kek religion,
   An' I'll kek ankair kennā,
But if wāver fóki kams lis,
   Mūkk lendy kair ajā.

Te mándy kek kairs pyáss
   O' sār ye wāver cháls—
If a chávo jāls to kāngri,
   Mā sávvy at léste, pals !

But sávo mándy pūkkers,
   Adóvo tácho sī,
O drom sī adré a geero
   Yúv sásti well avrī.

Dói's Charlie o Rashiméngro—
   Te 'cóvo mándy'll pen,
Ke, mūkk kāngréski cóvvar
   De mūsh sī táchipen.

Yúv rākkela troosal de Scripturs,
　Jinélla sār sī adré :
Tu'd pátser lendy tácho,
　To shūn o' lis del apré.

Adré o heb, yúv pūkkers,
　A chóveno kínyo mūsh
Can hatch apré, te múscros
　Te vel kékker kair lis dúsh.

Āwer i chálor so hócker,
　Te pī te sóvahāl,
Te vel kékker mūkkdo adré lis,
　Sā mán te vel kék'ra jāl.

Āwer, sīg as a wéshni-jūckal
　Te vel hūkker a káni avri,
Kún Charlie's rātt sī tátto
　Avélla o Rómmani.

Lis díckdom awāver rāti—
　Ghiom kéti lis kér to besh,
Te gáver pāli a chíngari
　Adré adóvo wesh.

Péndas yuv : "Mi pūkkdom tūkey
　Te 'dóvo to lel you dūkk,
O wéshni-kāni-chórin
　'Vel rig yer men to the rūkk."

Te hótchi : " So sos tu kairin ?
Fordía wafropen ! "
Te pánderdas i hevéngror
An' riggered de pīopen.

"Mi ghiom avrī," mi péndum
Talé the dūd adói,
To dickav a weshni káni
Or rúdder for yeck shoshói.

" Te dickum weshéngror wéllin,
An' chūried apré a rūkk ; "——
Pens yúv, " Midúvel fordé lis,
For a wālin o' wrath an' dūkk ! "

" Yol ródderdé 'pré a bíttus,
Te jāllan—āvo, sōr
But yeck : "——pens pūro Charlie,
" Yúv's tráshipen bā, to chore ! "

"Sār the dūd o' the chone apré lis,
Mi dicks so léste sī :
O rátfelo wéshéngro
So man' kairdas sā wāffodi.

" Yúv násti kaired a warmint
Kek wáfrodīro, bā ;
The beng ! "——pens pūro Charlie,
" Mā sóvahāl ajā."

" I yāgéngri, mi dicked lis
   Talé i rūkkor chiv,
Te hóckered sā sīg apré lis,
   It tráshered him out of his jív.

" Mi léldom' is 'dré mi wástor,
   Te pet it atūt his zī,
Te pendom : ' Pūkéssa a lávus,
   Mārāva tūt' sīg avrī.'

" Yúv hátchdas apré sār pūk'no,
   Te kékera léllas kek trásh,
Sā yāgéngri sos chído
   Atūt his mūi, pāsh.

" Penāva mi : ' S'up mi Dúvel,
   Shan bōro sīg o zī !
Del lávus kek to slommer,
   Mūkkāva tūt' jāl avrī.'

" Yúv pūkkers : ' I'll kair my būtsi,
   Tho' I jins you've lélled mi, pal !
Āwer mūkerav' tūte práster,
   Te mán'y'll wéll palál.'

" Sā díom lis o yāgéngri,
   Te chindom sims dívio ;
Te shom akai ! "——pens Charlie,
   " M'Aráunyo párraco !

M

" Āwer, te lis sos a-mengy,
  Lis kékkera mūkdom jā,
Léldom mi o beng's yāgéngri,
  Te póggered his hérror, bā !"

E. H. PALMER.

——o——

I DON'T know much of religion,
　And I ain't a goin' to learn ;
But if any one takes up with it,
　That there is his own concern.

I'm not the kind of party
　As allus goes in for chaff ;
If a man *does* go to meetin',
　What call have you to laugh ?

But what I do maintain is,
　However much you try,
The ways as you've once got in yer
　Must come out by and by.

Now there's old Preachin' Charlie—
　And this I'm bound to say,
There's no one, barrin' his prayin',
　More honest than Charlie Gray.

He's learnt to read, has Charlie,
And spelt the Scripture through ;
And to hear him talk about it,
You'd half believe it's true.

And he says as how in heaven
The weary are at peace,
An' the wicked cease from troublin',
An' they don't keep no police.

But he says as how to git there,
You mustn't lie nor drink ;
And as that's agin all natur',
They wont see *me*, I think.

But a fox'll show his breedin'
If there's ever a hen about ;
So whenever you riles old Charlie,
His Rommany blood comes out.

The other night I see him ;
I went to his house to hide,
For I'd had a bit of a shindy
On yonder cover side.

Says he, " I allus warned you,
But it ain't a bit of use ;
Them poachin' tricks you're up to
Will get your neck in a noose."

Says he, " What *were* you arter ?
    The Lord forgive your sin ! "
And he fastened up the shutters,
    And fetched me out the gin.

Says I, " I was out by moonlight
    A lookin' about for a hare,
Or a rabbit or two, or a pheasant,
    Or mebbe to set a snare.

" But I see the keepers comin',
    And clambered up a tree ; "——
Says Charlie, " May God forgive you !
    What a wessel o' wrath you be ! "

" Well, they hunted about for a little,
    Then all went off but one,
Who stopped behind : "——Says Charlie,
    " What risks them poachers run ! "

" Then the moonlight shone upon him,
    And who do you think I see,
But the werry self-same ranger
    As allus was down on me.

" If I'd a been so much varmint,
    He couldn't ha' served me worse ;
The—— ! " " Can't you talk," says Charlie,
    " Without a hoath or a curse ? "

" Well, arter a bit he rested
  His gun agin a stump,
And down I come upon him,
  So sudden it made him jump.

" And I took and snatched the gun up,
  And put it agin his head ;
Says I, ' You shout or holloa,
  And you're as good as dead ! '

" He never moved a muscle,
  And I never see him flinch,
Tho' the muzzle touched his forehead
  Within a half an inch !

" Says I, ' You are a plucked un
  And no mistake—and so
If you promise not to follow,
  Hang me ! but I'll let you go.'

" Says he, ' I'll do my duty,
  Though I knows I am in your power :
But I don't mind if I give you
  A start of a half an hour.'

" So I hands him back his weapon,
  And cuts away like mad ;
And here I am ! "——Says Charlie,
  " Thank heaven you're safe, my lad !

" But if *I* had had the handlin'
That gun instead of you,
I'd a taken the butt-end on it,
And smashed his legs in two ! "

E. H. PALMER.

This story is told as it was related to a friend by a very
well-known Gipsy ; or, I should say, as it was very naïvely
told by the preacher himself. He began the narrative in a
highly moral tone, but, becoming excited, ended in the words
of the last verse.

# *I RÁNI TE O RYE.*

—o—

HAVING read to an English Gipsy a German Rommany song, given by R. Liebich (*Die Zigeuner*, Leipzig, 1863), he promptly translated it into his own dialect. The original is as follows. The Latin version is by Dr Fr. Miklosich (*Über die Mundarten und die Wanderungen der Zigeuner Europas*, Wien, 1873).

ĈAKERVELA i rani rajes peskere balensa
*Tegit domina dominum suis crinibus.*

I gadze pal o wuder tarde
*Homines post januam stant.*

Kamena te dikena me.
*Volunt ut videant me.*

Ho gerena kettené
*Quid faciamus una*

Me mūkkava tute nit.
*Ego dimitto te non*

Kostela es gleich mīro maropenn
*Etiamsi stet mea morte.*

Te hi tut' efta prála
*Si sunt tibi septem fratres.*

Te kéllela mīro dzi
*Si saltat mea vita,*

Ap o lengero charo.
*In eorum gladio,*

Tu hal miri te atchaha miri.
*Tu es mea, et manebis mea.*

# THE LADY AND THE LORD.

——0——

*ENGLISH ROMMANY.*

1 RĀNI shākerella o ryc sār péskri bállor,
"I górgior shan tárderin péller the wūder.
Kāmena ta díkk mándy.
Ko káiren mén kéttene?"
"Mi'll net mūkkav tūte
If it kosts méngy mīro míraben.
Shan tūkey héfta prālor,
Te mīro zi kéllela,
Apré léngeris hārro,
Tu shán mīri te atcha mīris."

*ENGLISH.*

THE lady with her flowing hair
Has covered her lover o'er.
"There are men who wish to see me here
Are hiding behind the door.

What can we do together?—
What canst thou do for me?"
" I will not let thee go, my love,
Though I lose my life for thee.
Thou hast seven brothers.   Though my heart
Should leap upon their sword,
Whilst thou art mine and I am thine
I ever will keep my word."

CHARLES G. LELAND.

O BŌRO divvúsko dívvus
  Ko sī adúvvel?
Kún tu sovéss' aláy
  Kéti bōro Dúvvel.

M. C.

TELL me what is
  The Judgment Day?
It is when unto God
  You dream away.

C. G. L.

# RÓMMANÉSKRO KÁMMABEN.

—o—

Oh, mándy shóm chōro té kālo ;
   Oh, mándy shóm kék pénsa rye :
Mā késsur chīchī pā adúllo—
   Mā késsur, mī Rómmani chi !

Oh, dīkkav o bōro kekāvi :
   Sī wáfro te kālo, we jin—
Āwer háder o hūb, mīri chávi—
   Shyán sī a káni adrín.

. Oh, díkkav adóv' hotchewítchi,
   Yúvs chúkko sī kālo ajā,
Sim spínyor, sā rūzno te nítchi :—
   Les' mās sī būt kūshto to hā.

Te vél tu sī rúmmado míshto—
   Te vél tu rúméssa sīgán,
Látchéssa ke mándy shóm kūshto
   Te sār mōri Rómmani shán.

JANET TUCKEY.

# GIPSY WOOING.

My face is as brown as a berry,
   You'd never take me for a swell :
But that will not make me less merry,
   So long as my girl loves me well.

That kettle is just like your lover :
   Outside 'tis as ugly as sin ;
But go now, and lift up the cover—
   Perhaps there's a chicken within.

And look at that hedgehog out yonder :
   He's ugly enough for a show ;
And his bristles, why, they are a wonder—
   And yet he's good eating, you know.

So if you will marry me early—
   So if you'll be gentle and true—
You'll find that I'll love you as dearly
   As ever a Gipsy can do.

JANET TUCKEY.

# *I CHÓVIHÁNI.*

——o——

MEN ghíom kéti givéscro kér,
I rāni sos pāni, te sím to mér ;
Āwer kána yói díckdas Rómmani,
Yói rākkerdas méngy kūshteni,
Te péndas, pāli o Sārishán :
" Mórélla méngy o chóvihān.

" Dickadói !—avélla kennā,
O wáfro cóvva kéllin ajā !
Midúvel ! Síkker ! "—Men díkkdom aláy,
Adói pāsh o wūder, díkkin adré,
Vás a bōro jómpa hóckerin án ;
Yói shélldas : " Adóvo's mī chóvihān !

" Sār-divvus, sār-óra avélla akái,
Te hátchel' apré, i bengéskri dyé.
Sī mándy chívāva o cóvva avrī
T'véla hóckerin 'pópli díckinav mī ;
Sā-rāti shūnāva lis pāli o tan,
An' sūtto sārjā o the chóvihān."

Ténna räkkerdum kétnes in Rómmani,
Te péndum akóvo ké mánūshi :
" Chív améngy bōro kátsas akái,
Te a cúrro o lún, mī kūshti chi,
Te sār o cóvva'll sī sīg sārán,
Kána méndi lelóva o chóvihán."

Simno trūsel i kátsas we lel,
Té o jómpa násti jā pīrri pādel ;
Āwer wáfro gúdlo lis shūndom kair,
Les jíndas ōra sī vel ta mér :
'Drína yāg sāri kátsas chídom lis án,
Te yói wūsserdas lún 'pré o chóvihān.

Kon i rāni das méngy mōro te mās,
Lévinor 'dústa te bállovás,
Te a kūshto pāsh-bár o' sónnakái :—
Ténna būtsi-mūsh sasto lél les wye.
Te tácho sī Rommanis wéll to tan
Vánka fóki lél dúsh áp o chóvihān.

CHARLES G. LELAND.

# THE WITCH.

—o—

WE went one day to a farmer's house :
His wife was so weak she could scarce arouse ;
But when she saw we were Rommany,
She spoke to us very civilly,
And said, with many a gasp and twitch :
" I'm dying—and all of a wicked witch.

" Look there ! look there ! It is coming now ;
The evil thing is dancing, I vow !
My God !  Oh, help me ! "—and peeping in
At the open door, with a wicked grin,
Came a great grey toad, with a hop and a hitch;
" See there ! " cried the woman, " see—*there's* my
    witch !

" Every day and hour it is coming here—
The devilish creature is always near ;
If I throw it away, the first thing I see,
It is jumping again and staring at me,
All night I hear it hiss by the ditch,
And all night long I dream of the witch."

Then we spoke together in Rommany,
And told her at last how the thing must be :
"If you have shears, just bring them here,
And with them a cup of salt, my dear,
And as sure as we're poor, and you are rich,
The Gipsies will soon take care of the witch !"

So we tied the shears like a cross, you see,
And held the toad—and it couldn't get free—
The charm was so strong—but it gave a cry—
For it knew that its hour had come to die ;
In the fire with the shears we gave it a pitch,
And she threw the salt on the burning witch.

Then the lady gave us all a treat,
Ale and bacon—plenty to eat,
And a ten-shilling piece as we went away—
Since people who work must get their pay ;
And it's good for all, be they poor or rich,
If Gipsies come when they're plagued with a witch.

C. G. L.

One fine day in Epping Forest I met a very jolly young
Gipsy woman, and held with her a conversation which was,
however, hardly to be called cheerful, since it turned princi-
pally on toads and snakes, with their relations to witchcraft.
In illustration of their evil nature, she told me the story
which I have repeated very accurately in the foregoing

N

ballad. I have no doubt of its truth, but would state, in explanation, that toads take unaccountable fancies to certain places, and even to certain people, and that the Gipsies, who were well aware of this, ingeniously worked on the morbid fears and superstition of the sick woman. In fact, the Rommany *chi*, after telling the tale, mentioned incidentally that "people who live in the woods as we do, out of doors all the time, see and know a great deal about such creatures and their ways."

Not wishing to be outdone, I signified my cordial assent, and promptly narrated a story which I had found originally in a strange and striking little ballad by a well-known American poet, R. H. Stoddard. There was once an old Gipsy woman, a witch. One day a gentleman going along the road accidentally trod on a great toad and killed it. Hearing a scream at that instant some way off in the woods, and after that a terrible outcry, he followed up the sounds, and found that they came from a Gipsy camp, and were lamentations over the old witch's child, who had just died very suddenly. On looking at the little corpse, he was horrified to find that it presented every appearance of having been trampled to death.

The simple credulity and awe expressed in the brown Gipsy face on hearing this little tale were as amusing as the puzzled look which succeeded them. She did not doubt the incident,—not in the least,—but inquired "*how* could it be?"—not being able to fathom the principle by which a soul could be in two places at once. I regret that I cannot report the discussion which probably ensued that night, around some fire, over this story, and the explanations given of it by the wiser and older fortune-tellers. It is not impossible that the next Rommany Rye or Gipsy-speaking gentleman who goes to Epping may, if he touch on the subject with due care.

be told the name of the infant thus killed, and learn many
interesting details of the subsequent effect of the bereavement
on its mother.

The word *chóvihān* in this poem should be correctly translated wizard, and not witch ; *chovihānī* being the feminine.

---

Tu shan i chóne adré o hev,
Mi déari, kāmeli rāni ;
Te wāver fóki shan o báv,
Kún gávla tūt' fon mán'y.

---

The moon, soft-moving o'er the heaven,
My darling, seems like thee ;
And other folk are but the clouds
That hide thy face from me.

# KÁMMOBEN, TÁTTOPEN.

—o—

"Mɪ shóm akónya," gílldas yói,
  "Men būti rūzhior,
Te sār i chíriclor adói
  Kair mándy gílior;
I mátchya 'dré o pánni súvv,
  O tem sī rīnkeno;  .
Āwer i jūva sósti rúvv
  Lella kék pīrrýno."

Givélla: "Wen avéll' akái;
  Shūnáv kék chir'clo gill;
I rūzhior shan sóved aláy;
  O dóeyav sī shíll:
Āwer tu shán pā mīro ríkk,
  Mi deari pīrrýno—
O kālo heb, o nāngo tem,
  Kennā shán rinkeno."

JANET TUCKEY.

# LOVE-TIME IS SUMMER-TIME.

―――o―――

" I WANDERED forth alone," sang she,
  " When summer flowers were young,
And birds made merry songs for me,
  The summer woods among ;
And gaily, gaily danced the rill,
  And balmy was the air :—
But there was something failed me still,
  Though all the land was fair.

" The blossoms all are dead," she sings,
  " That graced the summer-time ;
And summer birds have spread their wings,
  To seek a softer clime.
The wintry sky is dark above ;
  The silent woods are bare :—
But thou art near me, oh, my love,
  And all the land is fair."

JANET TUCKEY.

———o———

" AVALI rýa, I dicked the Shah,"
  Pénned ye pūri Petuléngerī.
" An I pens my chávo, ' Mā rākker ajā,
  For I jin yuv's a bitt' o' a Rómmanī.'

" Mándy jins sār sórtis o' Rómmanis,
  Mórnis te wāver-témmeny :
I jins lens yākkor an' jāvomus,
  I pens you adóvvo's a Rómmanī.

" Górgiki yākkor shán kūshti ajā,
  Né penāva shan kek rínkenī ;
Awer mándy penāva the yākk o' the Shah
  Bitcher the dūd o' the Rómmanī."

An' as mándy shūned lākis rākkerben,
  Yeck láv adré trin sos Fársanī ;
It sims yói pūkkerdas táchopen,
  And the Shāh sos a bitt' o' a Rommanī.

CHARLES G. LELAND.

# THE SHAH.

———o———

"YES, my master, I've seen the Shah,"
    Said old Dame Petulengro to me.
"And I says to my son, 'You needn't talk,
    For I know he's a bit of a Rommany.'

"I've seen all sorts of Gipsy folk,
    Our own and them from beyond the sea;
I knows the eye, and I knows the walk :
    I tell you he's somehow a Rommany.

"Other folks' eyes may be werry good eyes,
    I won't say never how *that* may be;
But this I say, that that Persian rye's
    Have got the shine of the Rommany."

And as she talked in her Gipsy tongue,
    With just one Persian word in three,
It seemed as if she couldn't be wrong,
    And the Shah were a bit of a Rommany.

---

The incident here described is true, every expression having
been accurately retained. No effort has been made to intro-

duce Persian words in these lines, and it chances that the proportion of them is rather less here than usually occurs. The
following, however, belong to that language : Avali, Persian
*bali;* rye, Pers. *ray;* räkker, Pers. *rakidan;* kush-ti, Pers.
*khush;* shuned, Pers. *shun-idan;* puri, Pers. *pir;* Mā (pro-
hibitative), Pers. *ma;* Gorgiko (from Gorgio), Pers. *kh'aja,*
pronounced *khorja.*

# GILLI.

—o—

*Of a Rómmany chi*
*Te a Górgio rye.*

Sī mándy sos tīro chávo,
   Sī tūte sos mīri dye,
Kāméssa dél mándy a chūmer?——
   "Kékker, mī rūzno rye!"

Āwer mī shóm kék tīro chávo,
   Āwer tūte shán kék mīri dye:——
"Adóva's a wāver cóvva;
   Āvo, mī kūshto rye!"

# SONG.

—o—

If I were your little baby,
   If you were my mother old,
You would give me a kiss, my darling ?——
   " Oh, sir, you are far too bold!"

But as you are not my mother,
   But as I am not your son ?——
" Ah, that is another matter,
   So maybe I'll give you one!"

# O PÁTTERÁN.

—o—

" TRIN mīa dūro pánni,
   Trin mīa dūro gáv,
Mi látchdom pátteráni,
   A cúttor lūllo táv :
Man díckdom sīg ye cóvva
   Sos tácho Rómmani :
A rákli lūkis shūba
   Lis chíngerdas avrī.

" Sos pándo pré ye rūkkor ;
   Te rūderin adói,
Mi látchdom 'pré ye pūvor
   A Rómmani patói.
Sigán ye dūi pīrried,
   O mūsh te pīrrýnī :
Amén a shél o' Górgios
   Jinás len Rómmani.

" Béshdom adói akónya,
  Te sār mán ásti díkk
Sos kālo, mūllo wóngur,
  Te pāno, mūllo chíkk.
Kái shán i dūi tāni,
  I Rómni te o Rom ?—
Andūro parl o chūmbor
  Shán násherdo adróm."

Mā dúsher, kāmeli, āwer,
  Ké yúl a-jíllo shán :
Yúl hátch kérātti wāver,
  An' látch a wāver tán.
I 'kāvi'll būller kūshto,
  O yāg hatch pālī án,
Te rákli'll chínger pālī
  A wāver pátterán.

Mā pátser kékker dúsher
  Fon wāver fókis dúsh.
Sār rákli léla ŗáklo,
  Sār mánūshi a mūsh.
Sī kékker yāg hótchélla
  'Pré 'cóvo tem kennā,
Āwer adré a wāver
  Sī kūshtidīr ajā.

CHARLES G. LELAND.

## THE GIPSY SIGN.

—o—

" THREE miles beyond the hamlet,
.  Three miles beyond the mere,
There hangs a shred of scarlet—
    The Rommanis were here !
Right well I know the token
    They leave where'er they stray :
Some Gipsy from her kirtle
    Has torn this strip away.

" It's fluttering in the thicket,
    And, as I search around,
I find the Gipsy foot-prints
    Upon the mossy ground.
'Twas here the Gipsy lovers
    Passed underneath the trees ;
Among a hundred Gorgios'
    I'd know such steps as these.

" I sit alone, sad-musing,
　For yonder on the sward
I see a few white ashes,
　And firebrands black and charred.
And whither have they wandered,
　The Gipsy and his love?—
Perhaps o'er far-off mountains
　With weary feet they rove."

Oh, sorrow not, my darling !
　Oh, grieve not for the twain !
To-night they'll rest them gladly,
　And pitch their tent again.
Again the kettle's singing,
　Again the coals will shine,
And from her skirt the damsel
　Will tear another sign.

Then never weep, my darling !
　So long as love is true,
Each maid shall find a lover,
　Each man a maid to woo.
And though no kindly embers
　Are blazing close at hand,
Be sure the fire glows cheerly
　In some more favoured land.

　　　　　　　　　JANET TUCKEY.

——o——

Àvo, rýa, sī a pūro cóvva,
Te kennÁ shÁn būti-dústa béshor
Ké man shūndom pūro dÁdas pūkker
'Pré i héfta Rāttéskri Pīréngri.
Sā yúv péndas te sā mÁn lis shūndom :
Sī tu lÁssa sóvahāl apré len,
Te adóvo sóvahāl sī póggered,
Héfta rūtti wéllÁn i pīréngri ;
Héfta rātti wéll te jónger tūte ;
Héfta rātti dikÁsā i héfti.
Āwer, rýa 'pré i hèfta rātti,
Yéck o' len te well tÁssála tūte ;
Wāstor pāli tīro men chívélla
Te mūnélla sīgÁn tīro gúrlo ;
Te adói lúllenā 'vrī arātti.—
Āwer, kai shūnéssa tūt' o' léndy ?

CHARLES G. LELAND.

# THE SEVEN NIGHT-WALKERS.

—o—

Yes, my master, it's a queer old story,
And it's many a year since last I heard it—
Since I heard the good old father telling
All about the Seven Night-Walking Spirits.
Thus he told the story—thus I heard it :
If you took an oath upon those spirits,
And the oath upon them should be broken,
Seven nights will come to you the walkers ;
Seven nights they'll come, each night to wake you ;
Seven nights you'll always see the seven :
But upon the seventh night, my master,
By the seventh spirit you'll be strangled.
Round your neck the ghost will twine his fingers,
Then upon your throat you'll feel them pressing :
Then they pass away into the midnight.—
But, my master, where could *you* have heard it ?

Charles G. Leland.

An old Gipsy once assured me that he had heard of the
Seven Walkers, as described by Sir W. Scott in the oath

sworn by the Rommany Hayraddin Maugrabin. Whether my informant was mistaken or not—and I do not think he would deceive me in Rommany matters—nothing is more likely than that such a superstition should have been preserved among Gipsies.

# LÉL TĪRO KĀM!

—o—

Sī o Rómmani mūsh sī kínlo,
   Sī a gry adré o stanya;
Te o Rómmani chávo's bóckalo,
   Sī a káni adré o gránya;
Shan Rómmani chálor trūshilo,
   Sī lévinor 'dré o kítchema;
Léla Rómano chīchī 'dré léskro fém,
Shan bárveli Górgior 'dré sūr o tem.

JANET TUCKEY.

## HELP YOURSELF!

———o———

IF the Gipsy man is weary,
   There's a horse in the farmer's stall ;
If the Gipsy child is hungry,
   There's a hen near the granary wall ;
If the Gipsy lads are thirsty,    ·
   There's beer enough for them all ;
And if there's nought in the Gipsy's hand,
There are wealthy Gorgios in all the land.

JANET TUCKEY.

# O DELABEN.

——o——

SĀ mándy ghiom adré the gáv,
  Vas a bōro rashái;
  A bōro rýe :—
Tū jinéssa o mūshis náv—
  Te kairdas rākkerben,
  Te pūtchdas délaben
  For o náflopen kér,
  A búnnerin there :
Te penāva : "Yeck dívvus te vel mán ta mér,
Sos kūshto adré a bōro kér !"
So I pākkers mi wást 'dré mīri pūtsī :—
Lelov' a rūppeny kālor avrī,
An' pels it alay. Rýe díckella me
Te "párraco tūte, *Rye!*" pens he ;
An ríkkerdas stardy ánerjál,
To akóvo kālo Rómmani chál.
Sī tácho. Yúv bóngerdas kókero,
Sims rýas to wāver rýas do.

CHARLES G. LELAND.

# THE GIFT.

—o—

As I was going along the town,
    Came a clergyman,
    A very great man,—
You know him by name, I'll bet a crown ;—
    And preached like honey,
    Askin' for money :
    He wanted some
    For a Hospital Home ;
And I said : "If death ever should come to
    me,
I'd like to die *there*—respectably."
So into my pocket my hand I poke,
And out a silver shillin' I took,
And dropped it in.   The gent looked at me,
And—" Thank you, *sir*, for your gift," says
    he,
To this here black-faced Rommany !

It's a fact.   He bowed himself, d'ye know,
As gentlemen always to gentlemen do.

CHARLES G. LELAND.

This was the account which a Gipsy gave me of an honour which he had received. In narrating the event, he acted it to life, with great spirit and intense satisfaction, ending with a profound bow, in imitation of the one bestowed on him by the clergyman. It may be worth recalling on Hospital Sunday that Old Windsor Cooper, the Gipsy, once gave his only shilling to the good cause.

———o———

Sóski adré de bítcherin kérs
    Kai 'dóvvo béshoméngros bésh ?
Būtider wáfropens they kairs
    Ké dívio jūckals 'dré o wésh.

Te 'dósta chóvany Rómmani chál
    Sī líno 'pré for kairin kek,
Te párl de pánni sásti jāl—
    Te mándy péskro jínav yeck.

Jinéssa Matthew Kāmlo, Rye,
    So náshe'd his jūva wāver wen ?
Sos lélled for chórinav a grai,
    Te bitchered trin bésh stáripen.

But—béng's the béshoméngros zī !—
    'Pré mīro pūro mūllo dád,
The mūsh as húkk'd de grai avrī
    Sī kek adré Mat Kāmlo's gád.

"Soski did mándy kékker pen
  Sī mándy jínned lis ?"   Shūn acái :
Mi shómas trásh o' táchipen,
  For *mīro* rom chóred 'dóvo grai.

" Yúv sásti síkk'rav *halibi*—
  Penned kek adói kún grai sos chóred ! "
Sos trásher léster kókero, Rye,
  O' násherin for a mūsh he'd mōred !

E. H. PALMER.

## THE INJUSTICE OF JUDGES.

THE judges come and hold assize
   In yonder court—but what's the use ?
They do more harm, sir, with their lies
   Than any mad dog broken loose.

And many Rommany lads there be,
   Who ne'er a bit of harm have done,
Are sent to jail, or over the sea—
   And I myself well knows of one.

You knows Mat Lovell, sir, of course,
   Who lost his wife some years ago ?
He's took for stealin' of a horse,
   And got three years for doin' so.

But—hang them magistrates, I say !—
   By my dead father this I swears !
The chap as took that horse away
   Ain't in the shirt that Matthew wears !

"Why didn't I give evidence,
  If I knew that?"—Ah, there's the rub!
I couldn't speak for the defence
  *'Cos my old man had done the job.*

"He oughter proved a *halibi*,
  Said where he'd been and what about!"
Poor fellow, ah! he durstn't try:
  *They'd hang him if they found that out.*

E. H. PALMER.

The incident in this poem is given almost exactly as it was narrated by an elderly Gipsy woman of the better class, in a little alehouse, in Cobham, Surrey, on the fair-day 1873. In justice to the Gipsy, it should be stated that the last verse is added to her story from an entirely different source.

———o———

Talé the shélni pátrinya
    Apāsh o the kítchemā,
Mándy rākkerdom pūri Rosa,
    Te yói rākkerdas sīg asā.

Kána-sīg yói pūkkedas shūkáro :
    " Mū rākéssa Rómmanis ;
Adói avélla o múscro,
    Te vel béngus shūnél' lis."

" Te vel shūnélla améngy.
    Sī chīchi o léster pem : "———
" Mū jin'sa tūte mi rýa
    'Sis chinger ye sīg of the tem ?

" Mán'y shūndom mi dádas pen lis :
    Tūte mān pénnis or chin ;
Te būti foki shán náshered
    Ājāfera rākkerin.

"Si chíndo adré the lílyor,
    Te sī kékena líno 'vrī ;
Len pánderénna tūte,
    Pā rākkcráv Rómmanī,—
Pa räkkeren, āra chínnen
    A lil adré Rómmanī.

" Tu sī a bóro rýa,
    Āwer tūl kennā tiro chíb ;
Sī a būti násherin cóvva,
    Mōro kālo Rómmany jíb.

                        CHARLES G. LELAND.

# A HANGING MATTER.

——o——

ONE morning in Epping Forest,
  Beside the alehouse door,
I talked with the Gipsy Rosa,
  As I often had done before.

When she whispered quick and softly :
  "Don't speak in Rommany,
For there is a policeman,
  Who can hear as well as see."

" But if he hears us talking,
  He will not understand :"——
" Why, don't you know, my master,
  It's against the law of the land ?

" I have heard it from my father,
  It may not be spoken or writ ;
And many have swung on the gallows
  For nothing but talking it.

" And it's still down in the law-book,
 And was never struck out, d'ye see ?
They may swing you off the cross-beam
For a talkin', much more for a writin'
 A book in the Rómmany.

" And though you're a gentleman truly,
 Don't go in the way to be hung ;
For I say it's a hangin' matter,
 This talkin' the Rommany tongue."

CHARLES G. LELAND.

I do not know whether the laws passed in many European countries making it death to speak Rommany were also extended to England, or if so, whether they have been repealed. That the Gipsies themselves entertain the opinion that their language is forbidden, invariably manifests itself, even if talking it with gentlemen or ladies, when a policeman approaches. Many a time have I heard the rapidly spoken whispered warning : " Mā rūkka Rómmanis, rýa—'dói vélla múscro ! Don't talk Rommany, sir !—there comes a policeman !" More than once during my researches I have received such a kindly-meant warning.

# TAN-ROMANESKRI GILIOR.

## TENT-GIPSY SONGS.

# TRIN BITTI RÓMMANI CHÁLS.

BY —— LEE.

——o——

YÉCK bítto Róm'ni chāl chūryin āp a rūkk
Chūry'd āp t' trūppo an' béshed apré a shóck.

Dūi bitti Rómmanis chūry'd āp t' rūkk
Yéck slommerin t' wāver as béshed apré t' shóck.

Trín bitti Róm'ni chāls chūryin āp' a rūkk
Slommerin yéck a wāver till they póggered 'vrī the shóck.

Trín bitti Róm'ni chāls pélled mūllo 'lay the pūv
Lénter dye wélled alángus ānkaired to rúv.

Wélled sīg ānpālī a bōro chóvihān
As káired sār the chávvos apópli jívven án.

Lénters dye hátched a rúvvin, lénters dye lólled a kósh
An del 'em all a kūrin for a kairin such a bosh (dúsh).

> *Chorus.*  Yéck bitto Rómmani,
> Dūi bitti Rómmani,
> Trín bitti Rommani chāls.

P

# THREE LITTLE GIPSIES.

ONE little Gipsy climbed a tree, and how?
He climbed up the branches and sat upon a bough.

    *Chorus.*   One little—two little—three little—oh!
          Three little Gipsy boys!

Two little Gipsies climbed a tree, and how?
One followed 'tother one who sat upon the bough.

Three little Gipsies climbed a tree, and how?
They followed one another till they broke away the
    bough.

The three little Gipsies all corpses did lie;
Their mother came along and began for to cry.

There came a great conjuror who saw them, and
    then,
He brought 'em all to life, boys, and set 'em up
    again.

Their mother stopped a crying—their mother got a
    stick,
And gave 'em all a whipping for a playing such a trick.

This song was repeated to me by one of the James's (half-blood), as composed by a Lee. He gave it in a very imperfect form ; but it did not differ materially from what is here printed. Since writing the foregoing verses, I have received another version of the ballad, which will be found on the following pages.

## DESH TĀNI CHAVIS DURIKEN.

——o——

DESH tāni chávis, all adré a row ;
What welled o' lénder tūte shall know.

Yéck tāno chávo was chívved up a rūkk,
Pélled to the pūv an yúvs neck 'us broke.

Dūi tāno chávo hatched apré his head,
Wery sīg ānpālī yúv was látchered dead.

Trín tāno chávo his lévinor drank,
An' wery sīg ānpālī was tássered in a tank.

Yéck tāno chávo—dūi tāni chavis—
Trín tāni chavis they are gone !

Shtor tāno chávo kélled himself lame,
Pélled alay a coal-hév an' was never dicked again.

Pánj tāno chávo was dickin at the rain,
An' wery sīg ānpālī méred o' thought upon the
brain.

Shov tāno chávo tumbled 'pré a log,
Adói yuv was hotchered to sindor 'dré the yog.

Shtor tāno chávis—pánj tāni chavis—
Shov tāni chávis we must mourn.

Áfta tāno chávo prástered from a dog,
An' wery sīg ānpālī was náshered 'dré a fog.

Oitoo tāni chavi was always at war,
Yéck dívvus yoi was náshered 'dré the tav of her guitar.

Enneah tāno chavo was kellin' with a match,
An' wery sīg ānpālī was mullered by a witch.

Desh tāno chávo, yuv was booti tall,
Playin' Punch and Judy was tássered with his call.

Áfta tāno chávo—oitoo tāno chávo—
Enneah te desh all are dead.

Then the Drabéngro kūred his wife,
An' shook the tāni chávis till sār wélled to life.

Desh, enneah, oitoo, áfta chávis all glad;
Shov and pánj chávis, dancing like mad.

Shtor trín chávis, standing on their heads;
Dūi, yeck chávis, growing like weeds.

Desh tāni chávis, all in a row;
What wélled o' lendy, kennā you know.

# TEN LITTLE GIPSIES' FATE.

—o—

TEN little Gipsies all in a row ;
What happened to them I shall let you know.

One little Gipsy climbed up a tree,
Fell down, broke his neck—there lay he !

The second little Gipsy stood upon his head,
And very soon after he was found dead.

The third little Gipsy drank up his ale,
And very soon after was drowned in a pail.

      One little—two little—three little Gipsies—
      Three little Gipsies they are gone.

The fourth little Gipsy danced himself lame,
Fell down a coal-pit, and up never came.

The fifth little Gipsy was looking at the rain,
And died soon after of thought upon the brain.

The sixth tumbled over a log into the mire,
And afterwards was burnt up to cinders in the fire.

> Four little—five little—six little Gipsies—
> Six little Gipsies we must mourn.

The seventh little Gipsy ran from a dog,
And very soon after was lost in a fog.

The eighth little Gipsy was always at war,
And she was hanged one day in the strings of her guitar.

The ninth little Gipsy was playing with a match,
And very soon after was killed by a witch.

The tenth little Gipsy, who was very, very tall,
Playing Punch and Judy was choked with his call.

> Seven little—eight little—nine little Gipsies—
> Nine little Gipsies all are dead.

Then the doctor whipped his wife,
And shook the little Gipsies till they all came to life.

Ten, nine, eight, seven Gipsies all glad ;
Six, five Gipsies dancing like mad.

Four, three Gipsies standing on their heads;
Two, one Gipsies growing like weeds.

Ten little Gipsies all in a row ;
What became of them, now you know.

These songs are simply variations of an old American ballad originally known as " John Brown's Ten Little Indian Boys," and which has been changed in England to " Ten Little Nigger Boys."

## THE RAUNEY ON THE TOBER.

———o———

THERE'S a rauney jessin on the tober,
There's rye jessin after her;
He would del all the louver
In his putsey if the rauney
Would beshtolay with him.
He pens : " My dear rauney,
You shall have plenty of vonggar
If you will jess with mandy :
For in the sarlow we will get
Rumoured, for that will be tatchey."

—o—

THERE'S a lady going on the road,
There's a gentleman going after her ;
He would give all the money
In his pocket if the lady
Would " settle down " with him.
He says : " My dear lady,
You shall have plenty of money
If you will go with me ;
For in the morning we will get
Married, for that will be right (nice)."

These songs, one of which has already been published in
" The English Gipsies and their Language," were repeated for
me by a Gipsy woman, whose husband, a Gorgio, wrote them
out at her dictation. This will explain the peculiarities in
the spelling.

# GILLI OF A ROMMANY JUVA.

—o—

Dic at the Gargers,
The Gargers round mandy !
Trying to lel my meripon,
My meripon (meriben) away.

I will care (kair) up to my chungs (chongs),
Up to my chungs in rat,
All for my happy racler (raklo).

My mush is lelled to sturribon (staripen),
To sturribon, to sturribon,
My mush is lelled to sturribon,
To the tan where mandy gins (jins).

# A GIPSY WOMAN'S SONG.

LOOK at the Gorgios,
The Gorgios around me,
Trying to take my life,
My life away.

I will wade up to my knees,
Up to my knees in blood,
All for my happy boy.

My husband's ta'en to prison,
To prison, to prison;
My husband's ta'en to prison,
To the place of which I know.

# PRONUNCIATION.

# PRONUNCIATION.

—o—

In reading or pronouncing English Rommany, as given in this book, the following rules should be observed :—

*Ā* or *ā* is pronounced either like *aw* in such English words as *law*, *raw*, and *saw*, or with a modification of the same sound as heard in *father*. Such words as *rātti* (night) and *pānni* (water) are frequently but incorrectly pronounced *rarty*, *parny*, on the same principle which induces the uneducated man, whether English or American, to extend the *a* to *ar*. In *āvali* (yes), and its abbreviation *āvo*, the *ā* is strongly accented, in a very characteristic manner. In *pāsh* (half, near, &c.), it is commonly pronounced like *a* in *wash*. In most cases *a* is sounded as in *Ann*, *add*, *ale*, *aloe*, &c., thus—

*Ánner* (to bring), pronounced as in *Ann*.

*Addúvvo* or *addúvvel* (that), as in *adept*.

*Aláy* (down). In this word the first *a* is sounded as in *alley*, the second as in *lay*.

*Avrī*, *a* as in *aloe*, or in *have*.

*A* in *chávo* (boy) is sounded as in *have*, and is short.

*C* is hard, or like *k*, before all letters except *e* and *i*.

*Ch* is the same as in *church*.

*Chal* is often pronounced like *chul*.

*E* is generally pronounced as in *men, hen ;* and *é* as in French ; *ie* like *ay* in *lay*.

*G* is almost invariably hard, but in a few words, such as *sig* (quickly, &c.), it has sometimes a very soft sound, as in South German after *r*. It then is between *g* and *y*.

*Ch.* In a few words—*e.g.*, *plochta*, a cloak ; *bacht*, luck ; *chushto* (*i.e.*, *kūshto*), good ; *hóchaben* (*hockaben*), falsehood ; *hochter* (*hokker*), to jump—*ch* has the same sound as in German—*e.g.*, *Buch*. But for this sound most Gipsies are. rapidly substituting the hard *k*.

*J* is pronounced as in English or in Hindustani. In the middle or at the end of a word it is sounded like the English *dg*—*e.g.*, *laj* (ashamed), which exactly rhymes with *Madge*.

*V*. Not to be confounded (as Gipsies often do) with *u* or *w;* is here pronounced as in English.

*W*, as in English ; should not be confounded with *v*. Most Gipsies, however, treat *v* and *w* as the same.

*Ū, ū*. Like *oo* short, or the Italian *u*—*e.g.*, *wūder* (door), pronounced *woo*-der (not *wood*-er). *U* unaccented generally follows the English pronunciation.

*O*. In the word "*Rommany*," *o* has a peculiar sound,

between *o* in *Roman* and *u* in *rum*. The same is the case in *dóvo, adóvo, adóvel,* and *akónyo,* which are pronounced much like *dúvvo* (as in *dove*), *addúvvo,* and *addúvvel.* This rule is far from being generally followed, but it appears to be correct and ancient. Some confusion prevails among different tribes in the pronunciation of *rov* (to weep), *sov* (sleep), but they are generally given as *ruv* and *suv*. *Cóvva* is like *cover* without the *r* final. *Lóvva* (money), often called *lovey,* has the same sound.

*Ī,* or *ī,* is like *ee* in *see,* or is pronounced as in French or Italian. *I, i,* without the *long* accent takes the sound in most cases of the same vowel in *it, ill, pin;* but it never is like *y* in *by,* or the same letter in *high,* except in *chi* (a woman).

The following may serve as a guide in reading Rommany, it being borne in mind that the *oo* is not so much prolonged as the juxtaposition of two letters in English generally indicates, nor is the *aw* quite so full as in *saw:*—

Oh tūte jins mīro kāko, rye.

*O tooty jins meero kawko, rye.*

O tūte jins léster nav.

*O tooty jins lester nav* (*av* as in *have*).

Yéck dívvus yúv pīrried sār lester gry.

*Yék dív-vus yuv peer'yd sawr lester gry.*

Fon yéck'eti wāver gáv.

*Fon yék'etty wáwver gáv.*

Q

Apré kāliko rātti sā's mándy sos jällin adré o wesh, múskro dūi bori rūkkor, man'y shūnedom a boro wafodo gúdli; te chommany pelled alay apré o pūv pāsh o mándy te dias avrī a boro shellaben, sims a béngalo cóvva. Penāva mándy : "Sā's dóvadoi ?" Mándy sos būti trásheno. Āwer o cóvva ānkaired to hākker and kell sims dívius; te mándy viom an' látched lis sos a tāno rātti-chíriclo that had pélled avrī fon léstérs tán.

PRONUNCIATION. — A-*pray* (*a* as *father*) *kaw*-leeko (*eeko* like *ico* in *calico*) *rawty*, saws *mandy* sus (*us* as in *fuss*) *jawlin* (*aw* short as in *falling*) a*dray* o wesh, *múskro* (as in *musk*) *doo*-ee *boree rookor*, *man'y shoone*dum a *boro wafodo gud*-lee; te *chúm*many *pelled* a*lay* a*pray* o poov posh o *mandy* te *dee*-ass av*ree* a *boro shel*-laben, sims a *beng*-alo *cuvva*. Penawva *mandy* : "Saws *duv*-va-*doy* ?" *Awe*-wer o *cuvva* on-*cared* to *hocker* and kell sims *divius* ; te *mandy* vee-ome and latched lis (as in *this*) sus a *tawno rawty-chirry*-klo that had *pelled* av*ree* fon *lesters* tán. (Broken dialect.)

The reader will find the following outlines of a Rommany Rhyming Dictionary, compiled by Miss Tuckey, of much use in acquiring the pronunciation and accents of the language. It embraces both the perfect and "allowable" rhymes.

CHARLES G. LELAND.

# DICTIONARY.

——o——

## A

Ajŭ, *thus, again.*
Asā, *also.*
Bā, *friend, companion.*
Dā, *give.*
Hŭ, *eat.*
Jā, *go.*
Kāmasa, *thou lovest.*
Kennā, *now.*
Krállissa, *a queen.*
Mollasā, *never mind.*
Paramīsa, *a fable.*
Sā, *all, so.*

Hŏra, *an hour, a watch.*
Ōra, *a penny.*
Kamŏra, *a room.*
Yŏra, *an egg.*

Adóvva, *that, those.*
Cóvva, *a thing.*
Lóvva, *money.*

Dányа, *a root, teeth.*
Gránya, *a granary.*
Kúnya, *a sack, bag.*
Ránya, *a reed, rod.*
Stúnya, *a stable.*

Kána, *when.*
Mánna, *to forbid.*

## B

Heb, *the sky.*
Chib, *the tongue.*
Jib, *a language.*

## D

Dūd, *light.*
Tūd, *milk.*

## E

Adré, *in, inside.*
Apré, *up, above.*
Shóre apré, *to praise.*
Alay, *down.*
Tuley, }
Tulé,  } *below.*

## H

Atrásh, *afraid.*
Bosh, *a fiddle.*
Kōsh, *a stick.*
Pūsh, *half, near.*

Bésh, *to sit, remain.*
Désh, *ten.*
Pésh, *to shine.*
Wésh, *a wood, forest.*

Hátch, *to stay, remain.*
Látch, *to find.*

Dūsh, dúsh, *trouble.*
Mŭsh, *a man or mouse.*
Rŭsh, *clean.*
Trŭsh, *thirst.*

**I**

Āvalī, *yes.*
Avrī, *away, out of.*
Bárvelī, *rich.*
Dílleri, *clever.*
Kétteni, *together.*
Krī, *an ant.*
Mee, mī, *a mile.*
Manŭshi, *a woman.*
Pī, *to drink.*
Pīrrýnī, *sweetheart (feminine).*
Rínkeni, *pretty, beautiful.*
Asti sī, *it is to be.*
Tácho sī, *all right.*
Sūmeli, *fragrant.*
Sūneli, *handsome.*
Sūnari, *golden.*
Sī, *is.*
Zī, *the soul, mind, heart.*

Dīli, *hearty, cordial.*
Gílli, *a song.*
Kílli, *to dance.*
Lūlli, *red.*
Mīli, *pleasant, kind.*
Mílli, *together, mixed.*
Nīli, *blue.*
Shílli, *cold.*

Dūi, *two.*
Mūi, *the face, mouth.*
Róoy, *or róy, a spoon.*

Kāni, *a hen.*
Pānni, *water.*
Rāni, *a lady.*
Sāni, *soft, silken.*
Tāni, *young, small.*

Akái, *here.*
Bai, *a bough.*
Chi, *a girl.*
Dye, *a mother.*
Gry, grai, *a horse.*
Kai, *where.*
Nai, *a finger-nail.*
Párakái, *this way, here.*
Ráshai, *a clergyman.*
Rye, *a lord, gentleman.*
Sónnakai, *gold.*
Wye, *due; to lel your wye, to get your due.*

Chīchī, *nothing.*
Hótchewītchi, *a hedgehog.*
Nítchi, *peevish, cross.*

Bítti, *little.*
Chítti, *little.*

Būti, *much, very.*
Nútti, *nuts.*
Tūto, *you.*

Dóri, *thread, rope.*
Kóri, *a thorn.*
Shukóri, *sixpence.*

Akói, *here.*
Adói, *there.*
Cóvakói, *this here.*
Dóvadói, *that there.*
Fergói, *a fig.*

Gói, *a sausage, pudding.*
Patói, *a Gipsy sign.*
Yói, *she.*

Férri, *to please, entice.*
Kérri, *at home.*
Pĩrri, *free, to walk.*

Chávi, *a girl.*
Kekávi, *a kettle.*
Lávi, *words.*
Névvi, *new.*
Sávvi, *to laugh.*

Kángri, *a church.*
Vángri, *a waistcoat.*

## K

Bāk, *luck.*
Lock, *shadow.*
Nāk, *the nose.*
Shock, *a bough.*
Tūlāk, *behind.*
Yāk, *an eye.*

Chíkk, *dirt, earth.*
Díkk, *to look, see.*
Flíck, *clever, adroit.*
Kék, *not, no.*
Ríkk, *side.*
Yéck, *one.*

Mūkk, *to let, allow, leave.*
Rūkk, *a tree.*
Tūk, *sad.*

## L

Aglál, ⎫
Agál, ⎭ *before.*

Ajál, *quick.*
Anerjāl, *opposite.*
Chál, *a lad, fellow.*
Drál, *through.*
Hāl, *to eat.*
Jāl, *to go.*
Pál, *a brother, friend.*
Pāshajāl, *neighbouring.*
Shimál, *the north.*
Sovahāl, *an oath, to swear.*
Trúshāl, *a cross.*

Dél, *to give.*
Ferdél, *to forgive.*
Kél, *to dance.*
Lél, *to get.*
Pādél, *across.*
Pél, *to fall.*
Shéll, *to call, whistle.*
Wéll, vel, *to come.*

Díl, *a wish.*
Díll, *quick.*
Jíl, *to go.*
Kíll, *butter, cheese.*
Líl, *a book, a letter.*
Níll, *a brook.*
Shíll, *cold.*

Dúll, *a declivity.*
Lūll, *red, the yolk of an egg.*
Mól, *wine.*

## M

Chám, *the check.*
Jā kām, *go slowly.*
Kām, *love, the sun.*
Shám, *the evening.*

Fem, *the hand.*
Pem, *a thing.*
Tem, *a country.*

Kim, *a side-tent.*
Sim, *like, resembling.*

Adróm, *away.*
Dróm, *a road, a way.*
Pīshom, *honey, a bee.*
Rom, *a Gipsy, a husband.*
Shom, *I am, we are.*
Viom, *I came.*

## N

Blán, *wind.*
Chovihān, *a witch.*
Drován, *quickly.*
Glán, *in front of.*
Grán, *a granary.*
Kān, *the car.*
Del kān, *to listen (give ear).*
Patterán, *a Gipsy sign.*
Sān, *silk.*
Safrán, *yellow.*
Sarán, *done, finished.*
Sārishán, *how do you do.*
Shán, *is, are.*
Sigán, *quickly.*
Shyán, *perhaps.*

Délaben, *a gift.*
Kālopen, *darkness, blackness.*
Kāmmoben, *love, pleasure.*
Kéllapen, *dancing.*
Lén, *them, to them.*
Mīraben, *life.*
Müllopen, *death.*
Pén, *a sister.*

Pén, *to say.*
Shíllopen, *the cold.*
Wén, *the winter.*

Adrín, *in, inside, within.*
Bín, *to sell.*
Chín, *to cut.*
Chín, *a blade.*
Jín, *to know.*
Kín, *to buy.*
Kín, *the edge.*
Sídderin, *drowsy.*
Trín, *three.*

## O

Būdero, *aged.*
Bárvelo, *rich.*
Bóckalo, *hungry.*
Chávescro, *a little boy.*
Chíriclo, *a bird.*
Dínnelo, *silly, foolish.*
Dóv ó lo, *what is that.*
Dūkkero, *sad.*
Kánavo, *half-blood.*
Kínelo, *tired.*
Mórriclo, *a cake.*
Náshedo, *hung, lost.*
Pīrrýno, *sweetheart.*
Pūkeno, *quiet.*
Sápeno, *wicked, i.e., snake-
  like, from sáp, snake.*
Sūvalo, *infirm.*
Trásheno, *frightened.*
Váccasho, *a lamb.*
Wáffedo, *bad, wicked.*

Avélla, *he, she, it comes.*
Brishinélla, *it rains.*

Péllo, *fallen.*
Shéllo, *a rope.*

Jíllo, *gone.*
Shíllo, *cold.*

Gúllo, *the throat.*
Lúllo, *red.*
Múllo, *dead.*
Túllo, *fat.*

Bālo, *pig.*
Kālo, *black, dark, lazy.*

Jíppo, *a patch.*
Trúppo, *the body.*

Chóvihāno, *a wizard.*
Pāno, *white.*
Sāno, *soft.*
Tāno, *young, small.*

Jáfro(ra), *such, as.*
Wáfro, *bad.*

Béro, *a ship.*
Kérro, *done, finished.*

Geero, *a person.*
Mīro, *my.*
Pīrro, *free, a foot.*
Tīro, *thy.*
Shírro, *sour.*

Cúrro, *a cup.*
Dūro, *far.*
Pūro, *old.*

Kérdo, *done, completed.*
Múrdo, *dead.*
Pūrdo, *hidden.*

Pīrdo, *half-breed.*
Pórdo, *full.*
Wárdo, *cart, carriage.*

Kūshto, *good, well, ripe.*
Míshto, *glad.*
Wīshto, *lip.*

Mātto, *drunk.*
Tátto, *hot, clever.*

Āvo, *yes.*
Chávo, *boy, youth.*
Sávo, *who.*

## R

Bár, *a stone.*
Bár, *a garden.*
Bár, *a pound (20s.)*
Chár, *grass.*
Gōgemár, *a swamp.*
Kár, *company ; kair lis in kár, do it in company.*
Katār, *rails, fence.*
Pūkūr, *aloud.*
Sār, *all.*
Sārasār, *always, forever.*
Shūkār, *easy, slow.*
Solivár, *a bridle.*
Sovār, *sleepy.*
Tussār, *to comfort.*
Utār, *the west.*
Uzūr, *by chance.*
Wafadār, *bad.*

Bōroder, *larger.*
Būtider, *more.*
Kair, *to make, do.*
Kér, *a house.*
Mér, *to kill, strike.*

Kékker, *no, never.*
Níkker, *to swallow.*
Ríkker, *to keep, hold.*
Síkker, *to show, help, secure.*
Síkker, *sure, certain.*

Chókker, *to shoe.*
Hócker, *to jump.*
Hókker, *to carry.*
Näkker, *to stray.*
Mäkker, *to defile.*
Pógger, *to break.*
Räkker, *to speak, talk.*
Shókker, *to yell.*
Stäkker, *to climb into.*

Dükker, *to tell fortunes.*
Lúcker, *to hide.*
Núcker, *to neigh.*
Pükker, *to tell, ask.*
Shúkker, *to shake.*
Süker, *to warm.*

Düter, *to rise (the sun).*
Lüter, *to steal.*
Jöter, *together.*

Gíller, *to sing.*
Hüller, *to carry.*
Lüller, *to yell at.*
Míller, *to mix, adulterate.*
Müller, *to kill.*
Shíller, *to shiver.*
Tíller, *to hold.*

Bósher, *to play the fiddle.*
Bósher, *to bark.*
Dúsher, *to vex, grieve.*
Kósher, *to beat.*
Násher, *to spoil, lose.*
Trásher, *to frighten.*

Anner, *to bring.*
Dan'er (dander), *to bite.*
Püder, *to blow.*
Rüder, *to clothe.*
Wüder, *a door.*

Késsur, *to care.*
Küsser, *to adorn.*
Nísser, *to swallow.*
Péssur, *to pay.*
Tásser, *to drown, choke.*
Wüsser, *to throw, fling.*

Láster, *to find.*
Práster, *to run.*
Wáster, *to hold, handle.*

Kíster, *to ride.*
Léster, *his, to him.*

Bór, *a hedge.*
Chóre, *to steal.*
Cór, *the edge.*
Lévinor, *beer, ale.*
Mór, *to kill, murder.*
Pór, *a feather, tail.*
Shtór, *four.*

Dür, *far.*
Gür, *the thunder.*
Kür, *to fight.*
Kúr, *outside.*
Lür, *to steal.*
Shür, *the beginning.*

## S

Jás, *he, she, it went.*
Jä päláss, *go behind.*
Káss, *hay.*
Lás, *he, she, it got, took.*

Léllas, *he, she, it took*.

Mäs, *meat*.

Näkelas, *was silent ; yúv näkelas, he never spoke*.

Péndas, *he, she, it said*.

Pyáss, *fun, a game*.

Syáss, *shade, shadow*.

Tás, *a cup*.

Vás, *he, she, it came*.

Lis, *it*.

Rómmanis, *Gipsy ; rākker Rómmanis, to talk Gipsy*.

Kéttenus, *together*.

Kürimus, *a fight*.

Pátserus, *possible, credible ; from patser, to believe, trust*.

Pūs, *straw*.

Pūvius, *a field*.

Sos, sús, *was, were*.

## T

Rätt, *blood*.

Tát, *total*.

Pát (cant?), *foot*.

Tom-pat, *foot*.

Skát, kát, *cut*.

## V

Av, *come*.

Doe'yáv, *river, sea*.

Gáv, *a town, village*.

Kür'hav, *a proverb*.

Láv, *a word*.

Náv, *a name*.

Sáv, *to laugh*.

Táv, *thread*.

Chiv, *to put*.

Hev, *a hole, window*.

Giv, *wheat*.

Jiv, *alive*.

Riv, *to put on (clothes), to dress*.

Siv, *to sew*.

Tiv, *to knit*.

Yiv, *the snow*.

Pūv, *a field, the ground*.

Súvv, *to swim*.

Tūv, *to smoke*.

Rúvv, *to weep*.

Yúv, *he*.

Shove, *six*.

Sove, *to sleep*.

Tove, *to wash*.

# GLOSSARY.

——o——

## A

acái, *here.*

acói, *here.*

acóvo, *this.*

addúvel, *that.*

adénna, *then.*

adói, *there.*

adóvo, *that.*

adré, } *in.*
adrée, }

adrín, *in, inside.*

adróm, *away.*

adúllo, adúl, *that.*

adústa, *enough.*

áfta, *seven.*

agal, *before, in front of* (jessed agal).

ajã, { *so* (*often pleonastic, as*
ajaw, { kushti ajá, "*good enough*").

a-jíllo, *gone.*

akái, *here.*

akónya, } *alone.*
akónyo, }

a lay, }
alay, } *down.*
alè, }

Alīsa, *Alice* (*a proper name*).

amándi, *we, us.*

amén, *among.*

améndi dui, *we two.*

áu, *on.*

anāva, *I bring.*

ūnerjal, *over against.*

Ánglatérra, *England.*

ānkair, *to begin.*

ánner, *to bring.*

anncrela, *it brings.*

ānpāli, *back again.*

auvias, *came on* (*perf.*)

ūp, *up, upon.*

apópli, *back again.*

arāti, *by night.*

asā, *so also.*

asārla, *so, thus, also, as.*

asti, *would have, had to.*

ástis, *can, possible.*

ásti sī, *it can be.*

atch, *to remain, stay.*
atrásh, *afraid.*
atūkno, *sorry.*
atūt, *across.*
áv, *come ;* avakái, *come here.*
āvali, *yes.*
avāva, *will come.*
avāva, *I come.*
avélla (vela), *he, she, or it is coming.*
avéllán, *they are coming.*
avénna, *they come.*
āver, *a comer, one who comes.*
avessa, *thou comest.*
āvo, *yes.*
avrī, *away, out of.*
āwali, *yes.*
āwer, *but.*

# B

bā, *brother, friend.*
bai (by), *sleeve, bough.*
bābalo-dye, *grandmother.*
bābus, *grandfather.*
bāk, *luck.*
bākelo, *hungry.*
bakengro, *shepherd.*
bākro, *lamb, sheep.*
bāktalo, *lucky.*
bállor, *hair ;* bal, *a hair ;* balno, *hairy.*
bállovas, *bacon.*
bālo, *a pig ;* bālor, *pigs.*
bālo,
baulo, } *a pig, a hog.*
bālor, *pigs (policemen).*

bar, *hedge.*
bar, *a garden.*
bar, *a pound.*
bar, *a stone.*
būri, bāris, *a snail.*
bāro, *great.*
bárveló, i, *rich (fem.)*
bau,
baw, } *brother.*
báv,
bāvel, } *air, wind, breath.*
bávelo, *windy.*
bávo,
bávol, } *wind, air.*
bavol, *dust.*
baz, *back, behind, open.*
beeno, *born.*
beng, *the devil, flame ;* o pūro beng, *the old devil.*
bóngalo,
bengóskro, } *devilish.*
bóngis, *the devil.*
bóngis his zī, *the devil in his heart.*
berk, *breast.*
bóro, *ship, boat.*
bósh, *to sit.*
besh, *a year.*
beshāva, *I sit ;* beshela, *he sits.*
beshdas, *he sat.*
beshdūm, *I sat.*
beshed aláy, *he, she, or it sat down.*
beshélla, *he sits, to sit.*
beshellan, *they sit.*
besherméngro, *one who sits, a judge or magistrate.*
beshin', *sitting.*

béshor (beshya), *years.*
beshtoláy, *to sit down.*
bíbī, *aunt.*
bikin, *to sell.*
bikināva, *I do or will sell.*
bīsa, *poison made from beans.*
bisser, *to forget.*
bítcher, *to send, to emit.*
bítcherin-kérs, *police or assize courts.*
bitcherin-mūshor, *magistrates.*
bitcher pādél, *to transport.*
bítti, *a bit, a little, small (fem.)*
bittider, *fainter, lower (voice), less, smaller.*
bítti-mullya, *goblins.*
bitto, *a bit, a little, small.*
bīván, *raw, uncooked.*
blan, *wind.*
bóckalo, *hungry.*
bónger, *to duck, bend, bow, dodge*
bóngo, *bent, bowed, crooked.*
bongo, *unwilling.*
booti, *very.*
bor, *a hedge.*
Bórgav, *Walton (proper name), literally Hedge or Wall-town.*
boried, *it weighed.*
bōro, *great.*
bōrodīr, *greater.*
bōro'in, *growing.*
boro-pánni tem, *the south (lit. ocean-land).*
Bōri kítchema, *grand hotel.*
bōri pāni, *the ocean, the great water.*

bosh, *a fiddle, to bark, noise.*
boshoméngro, *a fiddler, a fiddle.*
boshto, *a saddle.*
brishin, } *rain.*
brishindo, }
brūno, *brown.*
būd, *after.*
būddika, *a shop.*
būdeskro, *a successor.*
būkko, *liver.*
būller, *to boil.*
būllerin, *boiling.*
búnner, *to shape, build.*
búnnerin, *building.*
būno, boïno, *proud.*
būt, *very, much, often.*
būti, *very, many.*
būtider, *more.*
būtidosta, } *plenty.*
būtadusta, }
būtiengro, *a workman.*
būtsi, būti, *work.*

## C

'cai, *here, i.e., acai.*
Cāmlo, *Lovell (proper name).*
cāms, *he loves.*
cáulo, *unwilling.*
cávacai, } *this, here.*
cávacoi, }
chai, chi, *girl.*
chairus (chýrus), } *time.*
chīrus, }
chal, *lad, a Gipsy.*
chalava, *I touch.*
chálor, *lads, Gipsies.*

chám, *cheek, leather, tin.*

chámor, *cherries.*

chámyor, *cheeks.*

chār, or chorl, *to pour out, vomit.*

char, *grass.*

chārāva, *I touch, vex, cover, wrap.*

chāro, *a dish, plate.*

chāvali, *boys, mates.*

chávey, *child, girl.*

chávó (m.), *boy, child.*

chávi (fem.)

cháv'or, *children — i.e.,* cháv-o, chav-ī, cháv'or).

chavorli, *here, children! mates.*

chávóri, *chicken.*

cheirus, *time.*

cheirusses, *times.*

chórus, *time.*

chi, *girl* (pron. chý).

chib, chiv, *tongue;* bōro aprè the chib, *boastful (great on the tongue).*

chichī, *nothing, fie.*

chikk, *ashes, dirt, sand.*

chidom, *I put, placed, stuck, laid.*

chidom, *me, I put.*

chin, *to cut, to write.*

chinamāngrī, *a letter.*

chingúrī, *a row, a quarrel.*

chinger, *through.*

chinger, *to tear, to scold, to quarrel, tear.*

chingaror, *sparks.*

chinnin peggor, *cutting skewers.*

chiriclí, *a bird (fem.)*

chiriclo, *a bird (masc.);* Rommany chiriclo, *the Gipsy bird —i.e., the water-wagtail.*

chiriclor, ⎫
chiriklya, ⎬ *birds.*

chīrus (*also* chýrus), *heaven, time.*

chitti, *nothing, trifling, little.*

chiv, *to put, place, fix, throw* ('vrī the chiv).

chiv aprč, *to put up, throw up.*

chiv avrī, *to put out or away.*

chivāva, *I do, or will, put, &c.*

chivélla, *he, she, or it puts, &c.*

chivved, ⎫
chido, ⎬ *put, placed.*

chókka, *boots, shoes.*

chommany, *something.*

chōne, *the moon.*

chóng, *a knee-joint, hill.*

chor, *grass.*

chōre, *a thief.*

chōri, *poor (fem.)*

chōrin, *thieving.*

chōro, *poor (masc.)*

chorredo, *not of pure Gipsy blood, stolen.*

chōvahāni, *a witch.*

chōveno, *poor.*

chovihan(i), *a wizard.*

chóvveny, *poor* (pron. chúvveny).

chūfa, *petticoat, skirt.*

chúkker, *to hit together.*

chŭkkered, *shod, booted,*
chúkko(a), *coat* (chúho).
chūma, *to kiss.*
chŭmbo, chumba, *a hill.*
chŭmbor, *hills.*
chŭmer, *to kiss.*
chŭmor, } *kisses.*
chumya, }
chúmmeny, *something.*
chŭnger, *to spit.*
chūrelo, *bearded.*
chūreno, *poor.*
chūri, *a knife.*
churya, *knives.*
chūrider, *poorer.*
churdo, } *a quadroon, not of*
chúrredo, } *pure Gipsy blood,*
(chur'do), } *also a poor person ;*
chúrredo, } *stolen.*
chúry, *to climb.*
chúrried, *climbed.*
chúrro, *a ball, i.e., a round object.*
chuvveno, *poor.*
chúvveny, } *poor.*
chúvvani, }
coonjerness, *secret.*
coor, *to fight, beat, strike ;* coora-
ben, *a blow, a fight.*
cóppas, *things, clothes, blankets,*
*tiles.*
'covo, *this* (*for* acovo).
cóvva, *a thing* (cúvva).
cóvvaben, *an incident.*
cráfni, *a button, a turnip, a nail.*
cúrro, *a cup, a tankard.*
cútter, *a bit, drop, rag.*

cútteréngerīs, *bits, pieces.*
cúttor, *bit.*

## D

díd, }
dádas, } *a father.*
dādo, }
dadósko, *or* dadéskro, *fatherly.*
dai, *a mother.*
das, *gave.*
de, *the.*
deari, *dear.*
déas, *given, gave.*
deep (*English*), *pure, accurate,*
*correct* (*language*).
deep-dīrus, *deeper, purer.*
deepodíridest, *deepest, purest.*
del, *to give.*
délaben, *a gift.*
del-apré, *to give up, to read.*
dell, *to kick.*
délled, *done, drawn.*
déllin, *hitting or kicking.*
déllin lescro, *" a givin' of him."*
déll oprè, *to give up, to read.*
dónne, *then.*
des, *gave.*
desh, *ten ;* deshtūri, 18 *pence.*
dick, *to see.*
dickamóngro, *a looking-glass.*
dickavit, *to see ;* tu sasti dickavit, *you should have seen.*
díckdo, *seen.*
díckdum, *I saw.*
dick kālo, *to look black or glum.*
dicklo, *a handkerchief.*

dícktum, *I saw.*

dick pálī, *remember (look back).*

díkk, *to wait, to see.*

dil, *a wish ;* dill, *quick.*

dili, *hearty, cordial.*

dilleri, *bold, clever.*

dínnelo, *a fool, stupid.*

diplus, *a dimple.*

dípplor, *dimples.*

dívio, ⎫
divius, ⎭ *mad, insane.*

dívvus, *a day ;* o bōro divvúsko dívvus, *the day of judgment.*

doeyav, *a stream, river.*

'doi's, *there is.*

dood (dūd), *light.*

dood (dūd), *a month.*

dórdī, *see there !*

dori, *rope or twine.*

dōrī, *string, cord.*

dóvalay, *down there.*

dōv' e lo, *what is that ?*

dóvo (dúvvo), *that.*

drúb, *poison, a drug.*

drábbed, *poisoned.*

drábber, *to poison.*

drabéngro, *a doctor, druggist.*

'dré, *in (for* adré).

dró his drom, *in his own way.*

drom, *way, road.*

drom, ⎫
dromus, ⎭ *way, road.*

dromya, *roads.*

droppi, *a drop.*

drúmos, ⎫
drúm, ⎭ *a roadway.*

dūd, *light.*

dūd, *a shooting star.*

dūd, *moonlight ;* taley the dūd, *by moonlight ;* div'sko dūd, *daylight.*

dūd-bar, *diamond.*

dūdikabin, *making a clean sweep of everything in the house, under pretence of pro- pitiating the planets ; a species of fraud often practised by Gipsy women.*

dūi, *two.*

dūi-dash (*i.e.,* dūi-tas), *a cup and saucer.*

dūiyav, *a stream, river.*

dūkk, *pain.*

dūkk, *spirit.*

dūkker, *to tell fortunes.*

dukker, *to pain, grieve, chide.*

dukkerben, *grief, trouble.*

dūkkerin, *telling fortunes.*

dūkkerin', *tempting.*

dūkkeripen, *fortune-telling, an augury.*

dūkkero, *sorrowful.*

dull, *a declivity.*

dūm, *back.*

dumbo, *a hill.*

dūmo, *back.*

dūr, *far, long, deep.*

dūrmi, *among.*

dūrodīrus, *longer, farther.*

dúsh, ⎫ *harm, hard treatment,*
dūsh, ⎭ *sorrow.*

dúsher, *to harm, injure, grieve.*

dusherári, *difficult ;* mā dūsher, *don't harm, don't grieve.*

dusheri, *hard.*

Dúvel-nasherdo, *God-forsaken.*

dúvels-pánni, *rainbow.*

dya, *oh, mother !*

dye, *a mother.*

dyéskri dye, *grandmother.*

### E

engri, *when added to a qualifying word signifies a thing, while engro is applied generally to an active agent.*

énneah, *nine.*

és, *it.*

ésti, *for sa esti* (s'asti).

### F

Fārsáuī, *Persian.*

fāshni, *false, counterfeit.*

fem, *a hand.*

fergoi, *fig.*

ferrī, *to entice, allure, to please.*

ferridíro, *better.*

fílissin, *a mansion.*

firstus, *first.*

flick, *clever, quick, adept.*

flicknor, *cleverer, quicker.*

fordé, } *forgive ;* Midúvel fordé
fordel, } lis, *God forgive him !*

fordia, *be forgiven.*

fordia wafropen, *may his sin be forgiven.*

fóki, *people, folk.*

fon, *from, away, out of.*

fotograféngro, *a photographer.*

### G

gád, *a shirt.*

garadom, *I hid.*

gargers — *e.g.*, Gorgios, *white people, not Gipsies.*

gáv, *a town, village.*

gavéngero, }
gavóngro, } *a policeman.*

gáver, *to hide.*

gavior, *villages, towns.*

gáv-mūsh, *a policeman.*

gávors, *villages, towns.*

gávver, garāva, *I do or will hide.*

gávvered, *hidden.*

geero, *a man, a person (especially not a Gipsy).*

ghias, *he went.*

ghióm, *I went, we went.*

ghión, *they went ;* ghilo, *gone.*

gil, } *to sing.*
gill, }

gíllaben, *a song, a singing.*

gillas, *he sang.*

gillóla, *he, she, or it sings.*

giller, *to sing.*

giili, *a song.*

gíllied, *he sang.*

gillior, *songs.*

ginner apré (g hard), *to count (also* kenner *and* kender).

Ginny pāni ; *Virginia Water (proper name).*

R

giv, *wheat, oats.*

givéscro, *a farmer, farming.*

givilī, *a song.*

giv-pūvior, *oat-lands.*

glal, *before, in front of.*

gói, *pie, pudding, sausage, &c.*

gorgiki, *English, not Gipsy (fem.)*

gorgiko, *English, not Gipsy (mas.)*

gorgio, *a white man, not a Gipsy.*

gorgiones, *in English.*

graior, *horses.*

gránya, *a barn.*

grásui, *a mare.*

grūv, *a bull.*

grūvni, *a cow.*

gry, *a horse.*

gúdli, *noise.*

gūdli, *sweetly.*

gúdlo, *a trick (masc.)*

gúdlo, *sweet, a sweet thing, sugar (masc.)*

gūjer, *to make a deep noise.*

gunno, *a bag, sack.*

gūri, *to make a noise.*

gúrlo, *throat.*

gúrni, *a cow.*

gurniáver, *a cucumber (b.d.)*

gūsveri, *wise, discreet.*

gūzno, *proud.*

## H

hā, hāl, *to eat;* hādom, *I ate.*

hābben, *food.*

háder, *to lift.*

háddered, *lifted.*

hādem, *we ate.*

hafta, *seven.*

hālaben, *a meal.*

hámil, *to attack.*

hāmlin, *kneading.*

hánik, *a well.*

hanser, *to ridicule.*

hāro, hālono, *copper.*

hatch, *to stand, stay, bring;* to hatch a tan, *to pitch a tent;* to hatch it, *to stand it—i.e., to endure it.*

hatched aprè, *stood up.*

hatchólla, *he, she, or it stands.*

hatchórdo, *stood, stayed.*

hátchin, *standing.*

hatch opré, *to stand up.*

haurini (hýno, húunalo), *cross, angry.*

hav, *come!*

hav acai, *come here!*

hav avrī, *come away!*

haw, *to eat.*

heb, *heaven.*

hófta, *seven (masc.)*

hófti, *seven (fem. and pl.)*

hekka, hekki, hokki, *haste!*

hórro, herrī, *leg, wheel.*

hev, *a hole;* coal-hev, *a coal-hole.*

hev, *a dimple, heaven.*

hevéngries, *shutters.*

hóvyor, *valleys.*

hovyor, *windows.*

hikker, *to confess.*

hockaben, *a lie, a fraud.*

hóckeni, *false, fraudulent, deceptive; deceit, a lie.*

hócker, *to jump.*

hóckerin, *springing, jumping.*

hóckerpen, *a lie, fraud.*

hono (hyno), *angry.* ·

hopper, *to carry away.*

hoppercore, *policeman.*

hōra, *a watch, hour.*

horra, *a penny.*

hotchélla, *it burns.*

hótcher, *to burn.*

hótchered, *burnt.*

hotchewítchi, *a hedgehog.*

hotchni, *whiskey.*

hōvalos, *gaiters, stockings.*

hūb, *lid, cover.*

hūfa, *a cap.*

hūkker, *to take away.*

hūkkered, *cheered.*

hūkki, *already.*

hūler, *to shelter.*

hūnkeri, *dry;* hūnkeri-rūkk, *a dry tree.*

húunalo, *bored, angry, bad, rotten.*

hunualo, *obstinate.*

hunnel, *to vex.*

hūnter, *to arise.*

hūnti, *get up!*

hūshti, *to rise.*

hushti apré, *get up.*

huski, *what for? why?*

hūter, *to hang up, to mount.*

hūtered apré, *got up (on horseback).*

hūtlo, *shallow.*

hūtto, *hung up, mounted.*

hyver, *to look into, to pry into,* "*peek*" (*American*).

## I

i, *she, they.*

indi, *firewood.*

is, *if.*

iv, *snow.*

.

## J

jā, *go.*

jafra, ajāfro, *as such.*

jāl, *to go.*

jāl, *to make to go;* jāl the graias, *run off the horses.*

jāla, *he goes.*

jālán, *go on! move on!* (*pron.* jollánn).

jāllau, *they go.*

jalls, *goes.*

jāmpa, *frog or toad.*

jau, *for* jā ān, *go on!*

jassed, *gone, went.*

jássin, *goin'.*

jāva, *I go, I will go.*

jāw, *go.*

jaw vrī, *go away!*

jelled, *went.*

jess, *go.*

jéssed, *gone.* ·

jessin, *going.*

jī, *to like.*

jian, *they went.*

jib, *language, speech;* drć savo jib, *in what language?*

jído, *living, alive.*
jíller, *to sing.*
jíllo, *gone.*
jin, *to know.*
jin, *to know;* jináva, *I know;* jindom, *I knew.*
jínaben, *knowledge.*
jínavit, *to know.*
jins, *knows.*
jíppo, *a patch, patched.*
jiv, *to live;* jiváva, *I live.*
jívabeu, *life, existence.*
jívvas, *thou livest, didst live.*
jívvin', *living.*
jónger, *to wake.*
jóter, jóta, *together.*
jove, *oats.*
júkala, *dogs.*
júkalo-Rommanis, *dog-Gipsy.*
júvo, } *a wife, woman.*
júva, }

## K

kai, *where.*
'kai, *e.g.,* acai, *here.*
kair, *a house.*
kair, *to do.*
kair lis iu kar, *do it in company with some one.*
kairáva, *I do, or will do.*
kairavit, *to do.*
kairdum, *I did.*
kair dúro, *to sink.*
kaired kin, *tired, sharpened.*
kairedo, *done.*

kairen, *they make, or do;* so kaireu meu, *what are we to do?*
kairéngeri, } *a house-dweller*
kairéugri, } *(fem.)*
kairéngro, *a house-dweller (masc.)*
kairéngror, *house-dwellers.*
kairin sig, *pretending.*
káj (kásh), *silk.*
káko, *an uncle.*
kal, *cheese.*
káli, *black (fem.)*
káliko, *to-morrow, yesterday.*
kalleri, *vain.*
kálo, *black (mas.), dark, lazy.*
kalódírus, *blacker.*
kálo drom, *a black road, dark.*
kálo pání, *the ocean, the dark or black water.*
kálopen, *darkness, blackness.*
kálor, *a shilling.*
kálo-rattescro, *appertaining to the dark night.*
kám, *the sun.*
kám, *business, affair, want.*
kám, *to love, like.*
kámakúnyo, *a mouse.*
kámáva, *I love, like.*
kámbri, kámli, *enceinte.*
kamóla, *he or she loves or likes.*
kámeli, *loving, lovely, enceinte.*
kámeli, *darling.*
kámésori, *loving, a sweetheart.*
kámésero, *lover.*
kámlidírest, *loveliest.*
kámlo, *loving, darling.*

kāmmoben, *anything agreeable;*
   tūkey kammoben, *for thy*
   *sake.*

kāmni, *enceinte.*

kamōra, kamōrus, *room (a.)*

kāms, *he loves, likes.*

kan, *the ear (pl.* kanawor).

kána, kán, *when.*

kangréski dromyā, *church-going*
   *ways, piety.*

kāngrī, *church.*

kāngrī-pov, ⎫
kāngry-pūv, ⎬ *churchyard.*

kāni, *a hen.*

kánuā, *now, when.*

kanner, *to stink.*

kánnīs, *hens, fowls.*

kánya, *a sack.*

kāp, *to take.*

kap, *to get.*

kap-būti ᴍᴜsh, *a prosperous man.*

kāppa, *clothes, a blanket.*

kār, *to cry out, roar, shout, call to.*

kāri, *a thorn, neck.*

karm (kām) *a gleam.*

káss, *hay.*

kasséngro, *a hay-stack.*

katsas, *scissors, shears.*

kauliko, *to-morrow, yesterday.*

kaulor, *a shilling.*

kaum, *to love, like.*

kávakai, *this here.*

'kāvi, *a pot, kettle (for* kekāvi).

kavodoi, *that there.*

ke, *to, that, as.*

kédi, *to pick.*

kédas (*i.e.,* kórdas), *thou didst,*
   *ye did.*

ke-divvus, *to-day.*

kek, *no, not, none.*

kekāvi, *a pot, kettle.*

kek cóvva, *nothing.*

kek-kek kūmi, "*not no more,*"
   "*never no more.*"

kókkeno, *none, nothing.*

kekker, *no.*

kekkūmi, *no more.*

kek nai, *not, there is not.*

kekūmi, *any more.*

kel, *to dance.*

kélled, *danced.*

kéllela, *it dances.*

kóllin, *dancing.*

kélloben, *a dance, a ball.*

kenaw, ⎫
kennā, ⎬ *now.*

kennā, *ago.*

kennādoi, *now and then.*

kennā sīg, *by and by, soon.*

kepsi, kípsi, *a basket.*

kópsi kosh, *willow.*

kór, *a house.*

kerātti, *to-night.*

kéravit, *to do.*

kerdo, *done, ended.*

kérela, *he, she, or it does.*

kérelo, *I do.*

kérimus, *doing, deed.*

kórin, *doing.*

kerm, *a worm.*

kerri, *at home.*

kerro, *done, finished.*

kessur, *to care, test, try;* mandy kessāva, *I care.*

kéti, *to, towards, staight to.*

kettena, \
kétteni, } *together.*
kéttenus, /

ki (*pron.* kye), *wherever, where.*

ki' and 'doi, *here and there.*

kil, \
kill, } *to play, to dance.*

kil, *butter;* kil-curro, *buttercup.*

killer, *to bloom.*

killin, *playing.*

kin, *to buy.*

kin, *the edge.*

kínlo, \
kínyo, } *tired.*

kissi, *much;* sār kissi, *how much?*

kíster, *to ride.*

kítchema, *an inn;* bōro kitchema, *grand hotel.*

klísin, *lock-up.*

klīsin, *to wind around spirally, to twist about.*

klisin, *a key, a lock.*

ko, *what.*

kōkeri (*fem.*), \
kōkero (*masc.*), } *self.*

kōk'ro—*i.e.,* kokero.

koin, *to love, like.*

kommeni, *some, somebody, any.*

kon (kun), *who, then, when, therefore, what.*

kor, *eyebrow.*

kōraben, *noise.*

kor'ben, *making a noise.*

korauna, *a crown;* pāsh-korauna, *half-a-crown.*

koredo (kurredo), *blind.*

koosi, kūsi, *few.*

kosh, \
koshter, } *a stick.*

koshter-stogg, *a rick of faggots.*

kosser, kusser, *to clean.*

krallisa, *the queen.*

Krallisas gav, *Windsor.*

Krallis'wesh, *Windsor Forest.*

krī-krīa, kīri, *an ant.*

krīli, *funny.*

kūder, *to open.*

kukalus, *doll, fairy, dwarf, goblin.*

kulla (kolla), *things.*

kúmbo, *a hill.*

kumi, *quiet.*

kūn, *who, when.*

kūneri, *old.*

kūnjerni, *secretly.*

kūnjī (koonjee), *narrow, close.*

kunsus, *corner, end.*

kūnter, *to adulterate.*

kūr, *to strike, beat, fight, to grieve, vex.*

kūraben, *a blow, a fight.*

kūraméngro, *fighting man, warrior.*

kūred, *beaten.*

kūrhav, *a proverb.*

kūri, *a cup, vessel.*

kūricus, *a week.*

kúrri (kúlli?), *tin.*

kúrran, *an oath.*

kŭrredo, *beaten.*
kŭrried, *beaten.*
kŭrsas, kŭrshni, *dexterous.*
kŭsher aprè, *to flatter.*
kŭshko, *good.*
kŭshkipen, *goodness.*
kŭshtier, *better.*
kŭshtiest, *best.*
kŭshti-rŭdered, *well-dressed.*
kŭshto, *good.*
kŭshto-bāk, *good luck.*
kŭshtodírus, *better.*
kúsno, *a basket.*

## L

la, *she, her.*
lab, lav, *lip, edge, profit.*
laj, *ashamed.*
lájipen, *shame, modesty.*
lāki, *her, of or to her.*
lākis, ⎫
lāk's, ⎭ *hers.*
lángs, *along.*
lasa, *her, with her.*
lássed, *he, she, or it took.*
lāstus, *at last.*
latcha, *to find, keep.*
latched, ⎫
latchdo, ⎭ *found.*
latchedém, *we met ;* lit., *we found.*
latcher, *to find.*
lāti, *to her, her.*
lav, *a word.*
lāva, *I do or will take.*

lavéngro, *a linguist, professor, orator.*
lávus, *a word.*
lé, *they.*
lel, *to have, hold, take, to own ;* yuv lólled a dróm, *he had a way.*
léldom, *I took.*
lóllas, *thou didst take.*
lélled, *taken, held, owned.*
lélled opré, *taken up, arrested.*
lélled adústa, *had enough.*
léllin, *taking.*
lóllo, *taken.*
lel rák, *take care !*
léls, *he takes.*
lel vin', *take care !*
len, *they.*
lénder, *them, of, from, or by them.*
léndy, *them.*
léngeris, *their, of them.*
lens, *their.*
les, *his.*
lóscro, *of him.*
lóskri, *of him (before a feminine noun).*
lessī (*pron.* les-see), *it is.*
lóster, *him, of or by him.*
lesti, *to him.*
lestis kókero, *himself.*
lévina, ⎫ *beer (German Gipsy,*
lévinor, ⎭ *löviua).*
lī, *it.*
līan, *ye or you took, got.*
līas, *he or they took.*
liom, *I took.*

lil, *a book.*

lilai, lilei, *lily, summer, maidhood.*

Lilengreski gav, *Cambridge (book-learners' town).*

līno, *taken.*

lis, *it, him.*

livinéngris, *hops.*

Livinéngri-tem, *Kent*

lívveua, *beer* (livena *or* levina, *probably more correct than* levinor).

lo, *he, it, that.*

lock, *a shadow.*

lódder (*pron. also* ludder), *to lodge, abide.*

loko, *heavy or light.*

lolo-pābo, *tomato.*

longo-dūro, *farther.*

louver,  
lovva,  
lóvo,  } *money.*  
lovvy,

lūchipen, *sensuality.*

lúdderin, *shaking.*

lūllan, *they vanish ;* len lūllan 'vrī, *they vanish away.*

lúller, *to vanish, disappear.*

lūlli, *farthing.*

lūllo, *red.*

lullo o' the yora, *yolk.*

lūllopen, *redness, ruddiness.*

lun, *salt.*

Lándra, *London.*

Laudraméskro jiv, *London life.*

lūr, *to rob.*

lūtfi chávo, *adopted son.*

lūtter, *to wallow* (lūtterin adré o chik).

luva, *money* (lovey).

## M

mā, *don't.*

mai (my), *I.*

maila, *a donkey.*

mā rūkker, *don't speak.*

mūl, mūlor, mūlya, *companions.*

malūna, *lightning or thunder.*

man, *I.*

mān, *musn't, don't !*

man, *the heart, soul.*

mander, *from me.*

mandy, *I, to me, me.*

mūng, *to beg, ask ;* mi mangav tūte, *I beg you.*

mūngerméngro, *a beggar.*

māno, *silly.*

mān pen, *mustn't say.*

mānsha tu, *cheer up !*

mansy, *with me.*

manūsh, *a man.*

mānūshi, *a woman.*

man'y, *e.g.,* mandy.

mūriklo, *cake.*

māro, *bread.*

māro's 'ker, *an oven.*

martadas, *he wailed.*

martāva, *I wail.*

mūs, *meat ;* Mūs-divvus, *Sunday.*

mūsker, *in the midst of.*

mūtcha, *a fish.*

mūtchka, *cat.*

mátchyor, *fishes.*
mátto, *drunk.*
mavi, *rabbit.*
mee, mi, *a mile.*
meeyor, mior, *miles.*
men, *among.*
men, *to me.*
men, *the neck.*
mendui, *we two.*
mengy, *me, to me.*
mér, *to die.*
méred, *died;* yoi'd a-méred, *she would have died.*
meréla, *he, she, or it dies.*
mériben, *death, life.*
'Mericanéskro, *American.*
mi, *I, me, my.*
midīri, *my dear.*
Midúvel, *God.*
mi duvvel's tem, ⎫ *heaven.*
Miduvelus tem, ⎭
mīli, *sweetly.*
miller, *to add up, to assemble, to mix, to adulterate.*
minner, *to make a fuss.*
minno, minnā, *my, mine.*
mīraben, *life, death.*
mīri, *my.*
mirís, *mine.*
mísali, *a table.*
míshto, *sweet, nice, glad.*
míshto pen, *sweet words.*
misto, *e.g.,* míshto.
mol, mul, *wine;* kālo mul, *port, &c.*
mol, *wine;* lūllo mol, *red wine, port.*

moléngrīs, *grapes.*
moléngri-tan, *vineyard.*
mor, *do not.*
mored, *killed.*
móriclo, *a cake.*
morno, *our own.*
mornis, *our own.*
mōro, i, *our.*
mōro, *bread.*
mortchi, *leather.*
'mout, *without.*
mūi, *face.*
mūi-engro, ⎫ *a likeness, a picture.*
mūiengri, ⎭
mūjer,
mūk, ⎫ *to let, to leave, to be worth.*
mūkk, ⎭
mūkk alay, *to let down.*
mūkkáv, *let go.*
mūkk mengy jal, *let me go!*
mūkker, *to fly.*
mūkkeran dūro, *flying far.*
mūkkered avri, *flown away, let out.*
mūkkered avrí his dūkk, *he delivered himself (liberavit animam.)*
mūll (mol), *worth.*
mūller, *to die, to kill.*
mūllered, *killed, dead.*
mūllerin, *dying.*
mūllo, *dead.*
mūllo, *a bubble, shadow.*
mūllo, *a spirit, ghost.*
mūllo baulor, *dead pig.*
mūllo chiriclo, *raven.*

mumeli, *light, candle.*

mun, *the forehead.*

mūnella, *he, she, or it squeezes.*

mūnjer, *to pinch, a pig that has died a natural death.*

muscro, *a policeman.*

mūsh, *a man, a mouse.*

mūshero, *masculine.*

mūshi, *arm.*

mútchiméngro, *a tanner.*

mútteriméngri, *tea.*

myla, *a donkey.*

mylas, *donkeys.*

## N

náflo, *ill, sick.*

náflopen, *an illness.*

náflopen-kair, *a hospital.*

nūk, *end.*

nūk o' ye divvus, *the end of the day.*

nai, *a finger-nail, there is not, non est.*

nūngo, *naked, bare.*

narkeri (nūkkeri), *spiteful.*

násher, *to lose, to hang, forget, spoil, run.*

náshered, } *hanged, lost.*
násherdo, }

nass, *away !*

nasser, *to lean on.*

nasti, }
nastis, } *it is not to, unable, cannot.*
n'asti, }

nav, *a name.*

návvo, *named.*

net, *not.*

nevvi, *new.*

nidderi (nūdderi), *ignorant.*

nik-būt, *no good.*

nīli, *blue.*

nisser, *to swallow.*

nisser the beng and sār jīvin, *to swallow the devil and every living thing.*

nisser, *to remove, miss, avoid, keep away, pour out, empty, extinguish, to vex.*

nisseri cóvva, *a strange thing.*

nitchi, *peevish.*

nok, *the nose.*

nōko, *one's own.*

nūtti, *nuts.*

## O

o, *the (masc.)*

oitoo, *eight.*

okki, okai, *there.*

opré, *on, up.*

ora, *or, (broken dialect).*

ovāvo, *the other, the next.*

## P

pū, *for, on.*

pū, *for ;* hatch pū leste, *wait for him.*

pū, *by, near, on.*

pābos, *apples.*

paiass, } *sport, jollity.*
paias, }

paiascro, *jolly.*

pákker, *to defend, to clean.*

pal, *a brother.*

pal of a lav, *accent (i.e., its brother, M.C.)*

pala, *oh, brother!*

paláll, \
páli,    \
palass,  } *again, behind.*
pále,   /

paller, *to follow ; to nourish, to rear.*

paller an, *follow after.*

palor, *brethren.*

pander, *to tie, to suspend.*

pandered, *tied, bound, close.*

panderpen, *the pound.*

panéngri, *a bell (corrupted into this form by an English Gipsy, who had at first learned it from a German Gipsy as* gam'pana.)

páni, *water.*

panj, *five.*

pánni, *water ; parl the pánni, over the water.*

pánser, *to approve.*

papiro, *paper.*

para, púri, *to exchange.*

par-akái, *before now.*

paravit, *split, shatter.*

parl, *over, across.*

parraco, *thank you.*

pásh, *by, near, beside ; a half.*

pásh-divvus, *afternoon.*

pásher, *nearly.*

pásh-ajúl, *neighbouring.*

pásher a pásh bar, *nearly half-a-pound.*

pásh-korauna, *half-a-crown.*

pásh-níli, *grey (half-blue).*

patói, *a sign.*

pátrin, *a leaf.*

patser, *credit, trust, believe.*

patserdo, *trusting.*

patsered, *promised.*

pátserus, *possible.*

pátteran, } *a track, a sign.*
patteráni, }

pauli, *behind, after.*

pauno, *white (masc.)*

pauni, *white (fem.)*

pauvero, *poor.*

peerdos, *travellers.*

peggor, *skewers.*

pekker, *to roast or bake.*

pelled, *fallen.*

pelled avrí, *fallen off.*

'pels it alay, *drops it.*

pelt alay, *fallen off.*

pem, *a thing.*

pen, *to say, to think.*

pen, *sister.*

peu (*a termination used in forming nouns, as* kushto, *good ;* kushtipen, *goodness*).

penáva, *I say.*

pendas, *thou didst say, he said.*

pendiom, *I said.*

pendos, *he said.*

penellan, *they say.*

pennas, *thou sayest.*

pennin, *saying.*

pennis, *a saying.*

pensa, pensi, *like, as.*

per, *to fall.*

pesh, *to shine.*

peskri, *her own ;* peski, *self.*

pessur, *to pay.*

Petuléngro, *Smith* (a *proper name*).

philissin, *a mansion.*

pī, *to drink ;* to pī your kām-moben, *to drink your health.*

pinder, *to attack.*

pingoro, *an associate.*

pīopen, *drink, something to drink.*

piredor, *travellers, walkers.*

pirólla, *he walks.*

pīrengri, *a traveller (fem.)*

pirengro, *a walker, a traveller.*

pūri, *a foot.*

pīrriben, } *a walk.*
pīrraben, }

pirried, *walked.*

pirro, *beginning ;* tācho pīrro, *well begun.*

pírro, *dear, free ; a foot.*

pírros, *feet.*

pirryin, *walking.*

pirryni, *dear, sweetheart (fem.)*

pirryno, *dear, a sweetheart (masc.)*

plashtu, *a red cloak, mantle.*

poggado, *broken.*

póggado zi, *broken heart.*

pogger, *to break.*

poggerólla, *he, she, it breaks.*

poller, *to feed, nourish.*

pooro, *poor.*

poov, *the earth, ground ; a field.*

pordo, *full.*

poréngripen, *writing.*

pōri, *a feather, pen, or tail.*

porno, *bacon.*

posserben, *burial.*

pov, *earth, ground ; a field.*

praio-tem, *heaven* (query, praller-tem).

prāler—*i.e.,* palor.

praller sherro, *overhead.*

prasser, *to abuse.*

prāster, *to run.*

prasterin o' ye gryor, *horse-races.*

'prè—*i.e.,* oprè, aprè.

pūders, *it blows.*

pūkk, *to say, to speak, to tell, to sing.*

pūkár, *aloud.*

pūkeni, *quiet (fem.)*

pūkeno, *quiet (masc.)*

pūkkelan, *they tell, they say.*

pūkker, *to tell.*

pūkkeras, *thou tellest.*

pūkkerin, *telling.*

pūr, *to change, to turn.*

pūraben, *a turn, the action of turning, exchange.*

pūreni, *old age.*

pūri, *old, aged (fem.)*

pūripen, *old age.*

pūro, *old (masc.)*

púrr, *belly.*

purūb, pūrus, *west* (Hindustani, the *east*).

pūs, *straw.*

pūsheno, *buried.*

pūsimegrīd, *spurred, pricked.*

pūsta, *a spur.*

putch, }
pútcher, } *to ask.*

pútchin, *asking.*

putsey, }
putsī, } *a pocket.*

pūv, *earth, ground ; a field.*

pūva, }
pūvor, } *plural of* pūv.

pūv-vārdo, *plough.*

pyass, *sport, jollity, fun.*

### R

rackli, *a girl.*

ráffer, *to descend.*

rak, lel rak, *take care !*

rākker, *to speak, to talk.*

rākli, *a girl.*

rāklo, *a boy.*

ran, *an osier.*

ránkni, *pretty* (Hindu, rangini, *gaily coloured*).

rāni, *a lady.*

ranjer, rúnjer, *to take off, undress.*

ranya, *osier twigs.*

rashái, *a clergyman.*

rasháior, }
rúshers, } *clergymen.*

ráshiméngro, *a preacher.*

rāt, *blood.*

rātfelo, *bloody.*

rāttéskri *nightly,* (*fem.*), *in the night.*

rattéskro (*masc.*) *nightly.*

rátfully, *bloody.*

rāti, }
rātti, } *night.*

rāni, }
rawney, } *a lady.*
rawni, }

religionus, *religion.*

rig (rikk), *side.*

riggur, *to take, carry.*

rikk, *side.*

rikk, }
rikker, } *to keep.*

rikker, *to carry, keep, retain.*

rikkered, *kept.*

rikkers, *he keeps, he carries.*

rikkorus, *beside, aside; the side of anything.*

rínkeni, *pretty (fem.)*

rínkeno, *pretty (masc.)*

risher, *to bribe.*

risser, *to turn, twist, &c.*

risser, *to tremble, shake, stir.*

riv, *to wear* (ridder, rūder).

rodder, *to seek, search.*

roi, rooy, *a spoon* (Hindu, doi).

rokker, *to speak.*

rokkerapen, }
rokkerpen, } *speech.*

Rom, *a husband, a Gipsy* (*Hindu,* Dom).

Romani, }
Romeli, } *wife* (*II.,* Domni).

Rommaneskas, *Gipsy fashion.*

Rómmaní chal, *a Gipsy lad.*
Rómmani joter, *the Gipsy gathering cry.*
Rómmanipen, *Gipsydom.*
Rómmanis, *Gipsy language.*
Rómmaní, } *Gipsy.*
Rómmano, }
romni, *a wife.*
rov, *to cry, to weep.*
róvades, *he wept.*
rovel, } *he or she weeps.*
rovélla, }
rūdaben, *dress.*
rūdderin, *seeking.*
rūdela, *he or she seeks.*
rūder, *to search, feel the person, seek.*
rūderpen, *dress.*
rūkestamengro, *a squirrel, literally, having to do with trees.*
rūkk, } *a tree, the gallows.*
rūkk, }
rūkker, } *trees.*
rūkkor, }
rummer, *to marry.*
rummered, } *married.*
rummoed, }
rūnjer, *to distress.*
rūppeni, *ambitious.*
rūppeno, *silver.*
rūsh, *clean.*
rúsher, *to attack.*
rūshni, *bright.*
rūvv, *to weep, cry.*
rūz, *day.*

rūzh o' the sāla, *dawn.*
rūzha, *a flower.*
rūzhior, *flowers.*
rūzlo, *strong, bold, harsh, stiff.*
rūzno, *strong, bold.*
rya, *oh, sir!*
rye, *a gentleman.*
ryeskro, *gentlemanly.*

## S

sā, *such, so, like, as.*
sā būti, *as much as.*
safrán, *yellow.*
sāko, *all this.*
sakūmi, *as ever.*
sāla, *the morning.*
sálamanka, *a table.*
sālivárdo, sāliváris, *bridle.*
sāni, *soft (fem.)*
sāno, *soft, thin, slender (masc.)*
sap, *a drop.*
sār, *all.*
sār, *with, as, like, how.*
sārapré, *all over.*
sārasār, *altogether, always.*
sār būt, *how much?*
sāridui, *both.*
sārishan, *how do you do? (for sār shan).*
sārjā, *everywhere, all.* •
sarlo, *morning.*
sāro, *all.*
sarrūti, *all night.*
sār'shan, *see sārishan.*
sā saf, *all right.*
sastis, *can, able.*

sasti, *perhaps, may be, must, should, &c.*

satcho, *true, truly.*

sáv, *to smile, laugh.*

sáveri, *cruel.*

sávo, *which, that;* sávo mūsh, *that man.*

sav' pen'la, *who says.*

sávver, *to laugh.*

sávyins, *smiles.*

se, *is.*

see, *heart.*

selno, *green.*

sensus, *since (b. d.)*

shab, *night, dew.*

shab o' the rātti, *to go by night.*

shaian, *perhaps.*

shāk, *body, bough, cabbage.*

shākerella, *she covers.*

sham, *evening.*

shām, *I am.*

shan, *you are, they are.*

shan, *bad.*

shūr-aprè, *to boast, cry up.*

shel, *a hundred.*

shell, *to cry or scream out.*

shóllaben, *a cry.*

shells, *he cries out.*

shelled, *cried out.*

sheróngro, 
sherróngro, } *head man, captain.*
sherréscro, 

shérro, *head.*

shérro-bār, *head-stone.*

shill, *cold.*

shilla en, *a cold.*

shilleri, *cool, chilly.*

shillo, *cold.*

shillopen, *cold.*

shimál, *the north.*

shindo, *wet.*

shīr avrī, *to pour out.*

shirkī, *star* (chīrikī).

shirro, *sour.*

shock, *a bough.*

shom, } *I am ;* shomas, *I was,*
mi shom, } *we were.*

shom shillo, *I am cold.*

shore, *to praise* (shār).

shorin, *praising, boasting.*

shoshói, *a hare or rabbit.*

shov, *six.*

shtor, *four.*

shūba, *a woman's gown.*

shūkār, *quietly, gently, dry.*

shúker, *to wither, fade, dry up.*

shūker, *to begin.*

shūl, *to whistle* (sholl, shell).

shūn, *listen.*

shūnaben, *obedience.*

shūnaben, *a noise, hearing; the sound of the voice; pardon; judgment.*

shūnalo, shūlo, *bad, ill-tempered.*

shūnela, *she hears.*

shūned, *heard.*

shūnelo, *I hear.*

shūns, *sounds.*

shūnum, *I heard* (tè sā man les shūnum).

shūveni, *beautiful.*

shyán, *perhaps.*

sī, *as.*

sī, *the soul, heart.*

sī, *be, is.*

siddi, *naughty.*

sīdus (zīdo), *alive.*

sīg, *quickly, straight, right.*

sīg, *way, manner, indication, sign, disguise, likeness, colour;* kek sīg, *no right.*

sīg, *or* sīk o' the tem, *the law.*

sīg, *to be;* sīg, *for, to pity.*

sīgaben, *a chance.*

sigán, *straight on.*

siggadīro, *quicker.*

sīg o' my zī, *anxious.*

sī kāmélo, *it is likely.*

sikker (sigger), *to shew, to teach, able.*

sikker, *sure.* •

sikkerūva, *I teach, shew, &c.*

sikkeras, *you teach.*

sikkerólla, *he teaches.*

sikkered, *taught.*

sikkerin, *teaching.*

sikkerin mūsh, *a teacher, schoolmaster.*

sīklo, *used to, accustomed.*

sim, *the same, like, to resemble, related.*

siménsa, *relations, kin.*

sims, *resembles.*

sindor, *cinders* (zīndi, *alive*).

sī pūsh sig, *perhaps.*

sīrán, *faster.*

sīro pūv, *a reaped field.*

siv, *to sew, a needle.*

skámmin, *chair.*

skūnya, *a boot.*

slom, *to follow, track.* ⁻

slommado, *followed, tracked.*·

slommer, *to follow, track (cant).*

so, *what, who.*

sónaki, *golden.*

sónnakai, *gold.*

soov, *to sleep.*

sore, ⎫
sor, ⎭ *all.*

sorno, *pork.*

sos, *is, was.*

so sī lis, *what is it?*

soskey's, ⎫
soski, ⎭ *what is, why, what.*

sossi, *what is it?*

sosti, *has to, must, ought.*

sov, *to sleep, to lie down.*

sovadum, *I slept.*

sovahūll, *to swear; an oath.*

sove, *to sleep, lie down.*

sovār, *sleepy.*

spínya, *a pin* (Med. Greek).

stūdī, *a hat.*

stani, *buck, stay.*

Stans Chūmber, *St Anne's Hill.*

stanya, *stable.*

star, *to imprison.*

stardī, *a hat.*

stūripen, *prison, imprisonment.*

starméskero, *imprisoned.*

staror, *the stars.*

starribened, *imprisoned.*

starya, *stars.*

stekka, *a stack.*

stigga, *a gate.*
süder apré, *hung up.*
süji (säji) dóvo, *what is that ?*
süker, *to burn.*
sükni, *hot.*
süm, *to taste, smell.*
sümeli, *sweet-smelling.*
süneli, *handsome.*
sünered, sünado, *left behind.*
sür, *deep.*
sürni, *bright red.*
sürrelo, *strong, hard.*
sürriko-müsh, *an actor.*
sus, *was.*
sütto, *a sleep, a dream.*
süv (süvi), *a needle.*
süvali, *infirm.*
süvo, *to sleep, lie down.*
snvo, *to swim.*
swishi, *ugly.*

## T

ta, *to.*
tácheni, *true (fem.)*
táchipen, táchopen, } *truth.*
tácho, *true, real, right.*
táchodiro, *truer.*
táchonus, *true.*
táder, *to draw.*
talé, *under.*
tämlo, *dark.*
tämlopen, *darkness.*
tan, *a place, a tent.*
táner, *to drown* (a *as in* Ann).
täni (*fem. and plu.*), *small, young.*

tänopen, *childhood, youth.*
tánya, *tents, camp.*
tarderin, *hiding.*
tás, *a cup.*
tasäla, *this morning.*
tasser, *to strangle, suffocate, drown.*
tassered, *suffocated, strangled, drowned ;* beng tasser tute, *devil strangle you !*
tátchi, *true.*
tátter, *to heat, fry.*
tátti, *hot (fem.)*
tátto, *hot (masc.)*
tátto, *handy, expert.*
tátto-kairaben, *sharp practice.*
táttopen, *heat, summer.*
tav, *string, strip, ray.*
tav 'apré, tav apré, } *to lift up.*
tawni, *little, young.*
te, *and.*
tel, *thread.*
tem, *country.*
ténna, *then.*
te vél, *to come ; used to express the future.*
te vél, *shall or will.*
tickni, *a child, a baby (fem.)*
tickno, *a little child, a baby ;* to lel a tickno, *to be confined.*
tikker, *to abide in.*
tikno, *a baby.*
tir, *near.*
tiro, *thine.*
titla, *a butterfly.*

S

tiv, *to knit.*

tívdas, *she knitted.*

tivved, *knitted.*

tober, *a road (a slang word.)*

toob, *grief.*

tool, *to hold, to keep, manage.*

tooled, *held.*

toolin', *driving (a cart.)*

toov, *grief.*

tove, *to wash.*

töver, *an axe.*

tövin-divvus, *Monday (washing-day).*

trad, *care;* lel trad, *take care!*

trash, *fear;* trasháva, *I fear.*

trásheno *(mas.)* } *awful, fearful.*
trásheni *(fem.)*

trásherdo, *afraid, frightened.*

trásherdo múllo, *frightened to death.*

tráshipen, *terror, a fearful thing.*

trin, *three.*

trindesh, *thirteen.*

trúppesko, *bodily.*

trúppo, *the body.*

trusháro, *a pannier.*

trúshilo, *thirsty.*

trúshni, *a basket.*

trúshul, *a cross.*

túfer, *to mend.*

túkey, *to or for thee.*

túkno (túk), *sad, woe;* túknus, *sorrow.*

túl, *to hold, to drive, squeeze, lead;* túl your chiv, *hold your tongue.*

tulúk, *behind, back.*

tulé, \
tull', \
tuller, } *under.*
túllno, /

túlker, *bitter.*

túllo, *fat.*

túneri, *fierce.*

túte, *thou, you.*

túv, *smoke.*

túv, *grief.*

## U

-us, *a termination often added to English or Gipsy nouns to disguise them.*

utár, *west.*

úzar, *by chance.*

## V

váccasho, *lamb.*

vánka, *when.*

vas, *he went, she went.*

vasi, *he or she went.*

vássavo, *bad.*

vasti, } *a hand.*
vast, /

váva, *will (affix).*

vías, *he came.*

vin (lel vin), *take care.*

víom, } *I came, we came.*
víom, /

vonggar, *money, coal.*

vóriso, váriso, *nothing, anything.*

vóro, *flour, meal.*

voudress, *a bed.*

## W

wādress, *bed.*

wāfli, *thin, scanty.*

wāfo, waffodī, } *bad, evil.*

waffodī jivvin, *bad or hard life.*

wāffodipen, *evil.*

wāfodi, *bad.*

wāfodipen, *evil.*

wāfodo, wāfro, } *bad, evil.*

wāfro-dickeno, *bad-looking (ugly).*

wāfropen, *evil.*

wālin, *a bottle, a vessel.*

wālin o dukh, *a vessel of wrath.*

wardo, *a cart, van.*

warter, *to watch, wait.*

wartni mūsh, *watchman.*

wast, *a hand.*

wasta-pord, *a handful.*

wasterméngris, *handcuffs.*

wastor, wastors, } *hands.*

wāver, *another, the other.*

wāver-temmeny, *foreign, belonging to another country.*

wāvero, wāvescro, } *differently, otherwise.*

wāvior, *others.*

welgora, *a fair.*

wellan, *they come.*

wellas, *thou comest.*

welled ta dukh, *"come to grief."*

well-gooro, wellgoro, } *a fair.*

wellin, *coming.*

wel, to wel, *to come; used to express the future.*

wen, *winter.*

wenésto, *wintry.*

wesh, *a forest, a wood.*

wesheugróski, *appertaining to forest rangers.*

weshengréski chōrin, *poaching.*

weshéngro, *a forester, a game-keeper.*

weshni, *forest, woody, wild.*

weshni drom, *the road towards a forest.*

weshni-jūkal, *a fox.*

weshni kāni, *a pheasant.*

wishto, *lip.*

witchaben, *hatred.*

witcher, *to hate.*

wóngish, *a little, a short time.*

wóngur, *money, coal.*

wóngur-divvus, *Saturday (pay-day).*

wórrisso, *anything.*

wūder, *a door.*

wūs, wūsser, } *to throw.*

wye, *due.*

## Y

yāck, *an eye.*

yāg, *fire.*

yāgéngro, *an inspector.*

yāgéskro, *fiery.*

yāgéskro chib, *a tongue of fire, flame.*

yāgni, *fiery.*

yāk, *an eye.*

yākim, *certain,* *i. e., marked,* observed.

yākk, *an eye, a wink;* to dell the yākk, *" to give the office,"* *to wink.*

yākkas, yākkor, } *eyes.*

yākkerpen, *eyesight.*

ye, *the.*

yeck, yek, } *one.*

yeck cóvva, *one thing.*

yeck'eti wāver, *one to another.*

yéckli, *only.*

yéckno, *one, single.*

yéckora, yókorus, } *once.*

yek pāl' a wāver, *one after another.*

yiv, *snow, ice.*

yog, *fire.*

yói, *she.*

yol, yul, } *they.*

yōras, *eggs.*

yuv, *he.*

yuv yūzhered avrī, *he cleared off, vanished.*

yūzher, *to clean.*

## Z

zī, *heart, mind, soul.*

zī-hūsh, *sensible, shrewd (Persian,* hush, *sense, shrewdness).*

THE END.

PRINTED BY BALLANTYNE AND COMPANY
EDINBURGH AND LONDON